THE
MINSTREL BOY

THE
MINSTREL BOY

Sharon Stewart

Napoleon Publishing

Cover art: Christopher Chuckry
Book design: Craig McConnell

Napoleon Publishing
A Division of TransMedia Enterprises Inc.
Toronto, Ontario, Canada

Printed in Canada

05 04 03 02 01 00 99 98 97   5 4 3 2 1

The author gratefully acknowledges
the support of the Ontario Arts Council.

Canadian Cataloguing in Publication Data

Stewart, Sharon(Sharon Roberta) ,   date
        The minstrel boy

ISBN 0-929141-54-7

I. Title.

PS8587.T4895M55   1997   jC813'.54   C97-931309-0
PZ7.S8499Mi   1997

TIME IS

TIME WAS

TIME IS NOT

–Sundial Proverb

TO RODERICK, FOR ALL THE REASONS
S. S.

PROLOGUE

He had always dreamed of fire. Flames flaring against a night sky and the dark figures of people running. With this, a sense of loss so keen that he ached with it. Then shouts, cries, and a searing blast of heat. A figure looming ahead of him, then a heavy blow that sent him spinning downward into darkness.

When he was small, he used to wake up crying. Now he was older. Shocked awake, he would lie in a cold sweat, aching with a loss he couldn't explain. Hoping not to sleep again before morning.

ONE

Bat-black night rushed at the motorcycle headlight. The road threaded through the valley toward the wild hills, and the lights of sleeping villages flashed by. The noise of his passing shattered the peace and quiet. David grinned and felt the wind against his teeth. About time someone stirred things up around here. Bloody Wales!

A signpost reared out of the dark at the side of the road. He wheeled around it for a moment, revving the engine. Caerleon he had just come from. And wasn't about to go back to. Not for awhile. Maybe a long while. Where, then? Usk? Abergavenny? Who cared, anyway? He chose the road that climbed.

Stupid. Stubborn. Selfish. His father's words hammered in his brain even as he tried to outrun them. It had been a monumental fight, one they had both been spoiling for. Well, he'd got in a few choice words he'd wanted to say. And he was glad. Glad!

They'd almost come to blows. With all the hateful words spoken, they'd stood glaring at each other.

It had been his father who had backed down. "All right," he had said, passing a hand through his hair, "let's cool off. We've both had our say. I can't seem to reach you, David. I know how hard it's been for you . . ."

"Oh, do you?" David sneered. "Do you really? I don't remember your ever being there for me. What did you care?"

"That's not fair, David." His father paused, reaching for words. "Things just didn't . . . work out between your mother and me. It had nothing to do with you."

"So you just walked out and left us with nothing." Remembering the hurt. Then, later, the shame of being poor, of having to wear old clothes to school. His naked yearning for the gear other guys had. His growing impatience with his mother's "crafty stuff," the pots and wreaths and wall hangings she made and sold to trendy shops uptown. They had brought in enough money to scrape by on, but no more. It hadn't seemed to matter all that much to his mother. She loved creating things, was proud that she kept the two of them going. But it had mattered to him. So did her oddness—her long, straight hair, the gypsy dresses she wore. She wasn't like other guys' moms. He'd loved her, but had wished she were different. It hurt to remember that now.

His father stared at him. "You could at least listen, David," he protested. "I said I didn't abandon you. I sent cheques, more than enough money to keep both of you going. She tore them up and mailed me the pieces."

"Good for her!" But he hadn't known that. Not that it mattered now. "So I guess that got you off the hook, huh? Very convenient!" he retorted.

His father shrugged. "Don't you remember how I used to phone? Ask to see you? She used to hang up on me. Then she taught you to do it." He paused to light a cigarette. "Anyway, what good does it do to keep harping on the past? Your mother's dead."

"I know that!" David snapped. And suddenly saw her face, thin against the pillows, her eyes enormous. And himself feeling frightened. Wanting to cry. Not being able to.

"Sorry. What I'm trying to say is that no matter what you think of me, we have to try to get along now. That's why I wanted to have you with me when I got the chance to teach over here. I thought we could make a fresh start . . ."

"Don't you think it's a bit late to barge into my life and take over?" David asked bitterly. "At least I had some friends back home. And I had my music." His voice choked up, and he hated himself for his weakness. "Not that you've ever understood that, or anything else I care about," he finished lamely.

"Oh, yes, your 'musical' friends." His father's voice hardened. "The ones you skipped school with. The ones who got so high on pills that they couldn't see straight. I met some of them the night you were arrested, remember? I still can't believe you were stupid enough to take any kind of drugs. And get into a car with someone who had taken them too. You're lucky the judge let you off so lightly!"

David scowled. He wasn't sure he understood himself why he'd gone along with the drugs. He'd said no dozens of time before. Maybe he'd just got tired of being the outsider. Needed to belong for once. And one of the guys had urged, "Aw, lighten up, Ice King. It's only pills.

Why don't you fall off your pedestal for once?"

So he'd said, "Yeah, why not?"

It hadn't worked, of course, not the way he'd wanted it to. The pills had built a spiky high inside him. Too high. It felt like climbing a mountain of broken glass. He could hear himself talking, babbling. Doing his thing with words. And the others laughing. But inside the bubble of words, he was still alone, as he always had been.

"As for your music," his father continued, "you're right. I don't understand it. It's a waste of your talent, and it leads you to mix with scum! Why do you think I brought you over here? I'm hoping that you'll snap out of all this nonsense!"

"Snap out of it? You're unreal!" David shot back. "After all this time, you just don't get it, do you? Music is me, and I'm it. Without it, I'm nothing. Like you." He headed for the door.

"Where do you think you're going?"

"What do you care?"

"David!"

He slammed the door behind him.

Without it, I'm nothing. David zipped up his windbreaker against the chilly spring air. After hesitating a moment, he jogged off, not much caring which direction he took. I shouldn't have said that, he told himself angrily. He'd broken his own rule. Never let anyone know how you feel inside. Not anyone! Not ever!

What would be the point, anyway? Nobody would understand. Oh, he'd tried to tell his mother when he was little. She had soothed him, saying not to be afraid, the dream was only a dream. What he couldn't explain was the terrible feeling the dream left behind. An emptiness, as if part of him were lost somewhere, and he couldn't find it.

No one else knew. Not even Jamie, who was the closest thing he'd had to a friend. And Jamie... His mind touched the memory like a tongue probing a rotten tooth. Gingerly. Turning up his jacket collar, he jogged on.

Jamie. The only kid who saw something in him. No one else thought either of them was much good, but they'd suited each other. They'd muddled their way through school, scraping by in class, bench-mates on third-string teams, beginning to eye girls.

Then one day David had started fooling around with a beaten-up electric guitar Jamie's older brother had dumped in the garage. That changed a lot of things, at least on the outside. Because David found out he was good. Very, very good. Good without even knowing how to read music. He didn't have to. He could feel it, think it, on any instrument he picked up, after a little practice. He could write songs and sing them, too.

He took a chance and entered a school talent show, and won. Then a guy who heard him knew another guy who needed a guitarist for a band that played weekend gigs and school dances. That was the beginning. From being a loner and outsider, he became someone who counted, someone others followed and flattered. And he had some money in his jeans. Not a lot, but more than he'd ever had before.

He'd let Jamie tag along, got the band to give him a

chance on drums. Jamie wasn't exactly a natural, but he did okay. And he never seemed to begrudge David the limelight. Or the girls. The great-looking girls. Cheerleader girls with fuzzy sweaters and glossy, bouncing hair. All of them wanting something from David. Something that he couldn't feel, though he wrote about it endlessly in his songs. Love.

The music and what it gave him should have been enough. But after the first thrill, it hadn't been. Something was still missing. Maybe that was why he...

David cursed under his breath at the memory. Why had he messed around with Jeannie? It wasn't as if she had mattered to him all that much. She was a nice kid, that was all. But that wasn't how Jamie felt about her. David had known it and had still gone ahead. Just because he was bored, and she was there.

I thought we were friends! Jamie's words, wild with hurt.

That had been the end of it with Jamie. Then David had only the others left—the followers and the wasters with nothing inside them, either. He wished he could make it up to Jamie somehow. But he knew he couldn't. Wouldn't, because he was too ashamed even to try. Anyway, it was too late now.

David stopped, panting, under a lamp post, his breath a cloud in the cold, damp air. He shivered. All very well to take off, but now what? Back home he could just head for wherever the band was getting together. And dive into music, his own personal painkiller. He rubbed his calloused fingertips on his jeans, itching for a guitar. If only he could plug into the biggest amp around and blast out sound! That always got the blackness out of him. For a while.

But in this hick town? Where could he go? There was a chippy on the corner, its windows clouded with steam. Someone came out hugging a parcel wrapped in newspaper, and he caught a savoury whiff of fish and chips laced with the tang of vinegar. The smell made his stomach rumble. But he couldn't eat here. His father would probably come looking for him, and it wasn't all that big a town. He had to get out, away, at least for a while. But how? He felt in his pockets. He had some money, but the buses had long since stopped running.

Then he remembered Hywel, a kid he knew at school. And Hwyel's motorcycle. David grinned. Hyw had been so eager to show it to him—something he could impress the Canadian kid with.

A few minutes later, confronting Hyw's bike in the dusty back shed, David hesitated. It was Hyw's pride and joy. Still, he probably wouldn't mind too much, so long as David did the bike no harm and gassed it up afterward. And if he did mind? Too bad. He shouldn't have shown David where he hid the key, then, should he? He touched one of the handle bars. It was ice-cold.

Where could he go? He knew no-one outside Caerleon. But he had to get away for awhile. Had to. And this was the only way. Unwanted, a thought floated to the top of his mind. Jamie would have understood how he was feeling. Hadn't he always?

Except once.

David kicked away the stand and quietly rolled the bike down the alley and around the corner. It roared into life at the first try. Once away from the town he speeded up, leaning into the curves, almost parallel to the road. Heading into the dark.

That had been more than an hour ago. By now he must be fifty miles from Caerleon. How much fuel had Hyw left in the bike, anyway? It would be stupid to get stranded miles from nowhere. To have to phone his father to pick him up. No, thanks! He must be getting near the top. Surely there'd be a village up here or at least somewhere to buy gas.

He swept on around a steep turn, then another, the road doubling back on itself in a series of snaky curves. Then he was over some kind of pass. He pulled up to look around. He turned off the engine, removing the helmet and wiping his forehead on his sleeve. Around him, the barren landscape of the high hills lay bathed in unearthly brightness. A horned moon rode high above a wrack of clouds. From far and away below somewhere came the deep murmur of water over stone. High on the left, the rocky bones of a great stone tomb reared against the sky. There wasn't the gleam of a friendly light anywhere.

David let out his breath in a whistle. "Spooooky," he said aloud. Then wished he hadn't, for his voice sounded very lonely in the brilliant dark. There was a soft whir of pinions, and something white swooped over his head. He ducked as it swept back over him, closer this time.

For a moment his heart rose into his throat. Then the thing swooped again, and he chuckled. "Hey, owl," he said, relieved. "Give me a break. I'm not your dinner. Go find a mouse!"

The huge white owl landed on a bush beside the road

and sat watching him. David pulled on his helmet. It was no use going any further. He'd have to go back. At least it was all downhill.

Then he saw a spark of light in the distance. There *was* somebody out there! The light wavered, then grew a little brighter. It divided and became two and three and four flickering points, then more. It looked like torches. The chain of lights seemed to be moving up out of the valley toward the ruins. Dimly, as from a great distance, came the faint sound of singing.

David snorted in contempt. Now, who would go wandering around in the middle of the night with torches? Singing, no less! Must be some crazy Welsh custom. He watched the lights for a few moments. Judging by the direction they were taking, they'd be crossing the road not too far ahead of him. Then, almost as though it had been put there, a thought popped into his mind. Why not zoom down on these yokels, just to remind them this was the twentieth century! And when he'd had his fun, he could ask the way to the nearest gas station too.

He switched on the ignition, and the bike coughed into life. "So long, owl," he said, looking around. But the owl had vanished.

As he bore down on the lights, he expected them to waver, to take note of his presence somehow. Whoever it was must surely be able to hear him coming! Stubborn, were they? Thought they owned the road? Suddenly he wanted to give them a real scare. Of course, he wouldn't really hurt anyone. He'd pull up in plenty of time.

He gunned the bike toward the lights. They were

right on the road now, and seemed to be flaring up, growing brighter. The weird thing was that he could hear the singing even through his helmet. Now the lights were all around him, but he still couldn't see anything.

Then he did. His last thought was, "Where'd that blasted tree come from?" Then he hit it.

TWO

When he opened his eyes, all he could make out at first was a white flower-like thing above him. A splitting pain in his head made him groan and close his eyes again. After a few moments, he sat up cautiously, holding his head. It was only then that he noticed the sharp, throbbing pain in his left leg. He groaned again.

The flower-thing was still there, except that now he could see that it wasn't a flower at all.

That wretched owl again! It was perched on a branch right above him.

"Yaaah! Get off, you!" he yelled, waving his arms. The owl just flapped one branch higher and stared down at him. He tried to get to his feet, but the movement made him so sick with pain that the ground heaved under him.

I can't just lie here! he told himself. Gritting his teeth, he managed to get his good leg under him and pull himself up, using a tree trunk for support.

Tree trunk? He gazed around, wildly. He was in the middle of a forest. All about him, great trees loomed in the dark. How could there be trees? He'd been up on the barren hills. Not a tree for miles. And even back home he'd never seen trees like these

11

giants, their tops lost in darkness.

Never mind the trees now, he told himself. You've crashed the bike, you stupid fool. You'd better find it! Painfully, he edged around in a circle, trying to keep the weight off his bad leg. He kept expecting to stumble over the motorcycle any minute. It couldn't be far away.

But there was no sign of the bike. Lovely, he thought. Lost in a forest, alone, can't find the bloody bike. Now what? He turned again, slowly, trying to pierce the surrounding darkness. As his eyes grew accustomed to the dim light, he thought he could make out a faint glow through the trees. He limped toward it, cursing as he stumbled over roots in the dark.

It took him forever to reach the light. When he got there, he found a campfire, neatly banked behind a ring of stones. Its ruddy-orange glow lit up a simple campsite. The camp was deserted, but clearly hadn't been for long. A rough blanket was spread on the grass, and a small stew pot of something savoury-smelling hung steaming on a crude frame over the fire.

David sank down on the blanket, and rested his head on his knees.When the worst of the pain had passed, he suddenly began to feel his hunger. It had been hours since he'd eaten. "Anybody here?" he called, but not too loudly. Surely, whoever's camp this was wouldn't mind if he helped himself to a bit of supper. After he'd been in an accident, and all. He found a piece of bark that had been used as a scoop and another that had served as a plate, and helped himself. The meat was nothing he could identify. It was chewy and full of flavour, well-seasoned with herbs and onion. David wolfed it down.

"Definitely beats McDonald's," he said aloud. "Could use a bit more salt, though."

"You're a very particular thief!" The voice was coolly amused, and coming as it did from right behind him, it scared him nearly to death. He struggled to get up, wincing at the pain in his head and leg.

Not three paces behind him stood a boy of about seventeen. He was tall and strongly built, with a mane of curly brown hair down to his shoulders. He seemed to be dressed up in some kind of weird costume. But the most noticeable thing about him was his sword. It was more than four feet long and looked sharp. And it was pointed at David's throat.

David raised both hands and began to talk very fast. "Hey, I surrender! That thing looks loaded! Don't carry weapons, myself," he said, feeling giddy. He took a clumsy step backward. The other boy followed, the sword levelled at exactly the same spot on his throat. Sweat sprang out on David's forehead.

"Say, I guess I shouldn't have eaten so much of your dinner," he babbled. "I just hadn't had anything to eat all day. And I had this accident . . ." His voice trailed away.

"You needn't apologize to me," replied the boy. "I'd had my fill. But you'll have to deal with Cabal. It's his dinner you've eaten." He gave a low whistle, and a shaggy wolfhound half as big as a horse bounded into the clearing. He stopped by the boy's side, every hair on his back bristling. A deep, ugly growl rumbled in his throat.

"Oh, swell," said David. "First I crash my motorcycle into a tree that wasn't there. Now I'm going to be sliced into pieces by a weirdo or torn to bits by a half-tame wolf."

The other boy frowned, as if puzzled, and the point of the sword wavered a little. "What is your motor . . . cycle?" he asked.

"You mean, *where* is my motorcycle. Beats me. Must be around here somewhere, but I couldn't find it in the dark."

"I asked what," said his opponent steadily. "Never have I heard of this thing."

For a moment, David couldn't believe his ears. Then, "Oh, go on and pull the other one," he snickered. "I mean, I know you Welsh are backward. But never heard of a motorcycle? Why, it's Hywel's motorcycle, actually, and he's as Welsh as you are!"

The boy's frown deepened, and the sword-point moved upward again. "What is Welsh?" he asked suspiciously. "Some insult?"

"Good Lord, no! I mean, would I insult you? With that thing at my throat? It's your nationality. This is Wales. You Welsh are the people who live here."

"This is Prydein. And the British are the people who live here," returned the boy. "Except," he added with a scowl, "for the cursed Saxons."

David began to feel sick again. British sounded all right. But Prydein? Saxons? The pain in his head was becoming unbearable. He reeled and felt himself falling forward. If I land on that sword, he told himself dizzily, my troubles are over! Then blackness took him.

When he came to himself, he was lying beside the fire, wrapped in the blanket. Across the flames, the boy sat whistling tunelessly between his teeth. His sword was sheathed, but he was whetting a wicked-looking hunting knife. The great wolfhound lay close beside him, his massive head wedged against the boy's knee. David must have made some slight movement, for Cabal's head swung up alertly, and he growled softly.

"Awake again, are you, thief?" the boy said. "You fainted."

David sat up very carefully. "I'm no thief, though I ate your dog's dinner. My name is David, David Baird," he said.

"What is this accident you spoke of, David Baird?" asked the boy. "Did you fall off your horse? Or out of a tree? I heard you blundering and cursing about the woods. That's why Cabal and I decided to circle around and have a little look at who was making all the racket."

"I crashed my motorcycle and hurt my head and my leg. And then I couldn't find the motorcycle again in the dark," said David. "I already told you that!"

"So you did. Well, we'll look for it in the morning. I've a fine curiosity to see it, whatever kind of a beast it may be. Will it wander far, left unhobbled?"

"Oh, give it a rest!" snapped David. He was getting tired of this game of pretend. "Of course, it won't wander off. It's a machine, not an animal!"

"From your mouth to my ear," the other returned calmly. "You should try to sleep now. That's the best cure for most hurts." He poked the fire, then looked up, his eyes holding David's steadily for a moment. "Though I may as well tell you that I had a bit of a look at you while you were out. There's no sign of anything wrong with you."

Gingerly, David felt the back of his head. There was no gash, not even a bump. He glanced at his fingers. There was no sign of blood. He looked down at his leg. It looked okay too—it wasn't bent or anything, and his jeans weren't even ripped. Why was he in so much pain, then?"

"I . . . I don't understand," he said, puzzled. "I hurt all over!"

The other boy shrugged. "It's best you sleep now, as I said. And happen you wake up, don't take it into your head to wander off. The Forest Fawr can be an unchancy place for strangers."

Rolling up in the blanket, David tried to make himself comfortable on the hard ground. Then he raised himself on one elbow. "I almost forgot. I've told you my name. What's yours?"

"They call me Bear," the other said.

"Funny kind of name," David mumbled, snuggling into the blanket. Then he noticed the owl again.

It was perched on a branch overhead, white as a lily in the dark. It ruffled its feathers, then settled them again.

"Drat that bird," David thought sleepily. Then, just as he was drifting off, he heard Bear speak to it.

"Lady of Flowers," Bear said, "I fear you've been a-hunting. But why bring your prey to me?"

"This guy is seriously weird," thought David, and then thought no more.

The grey light of morning woke David. At first he stared up blankly, wondering where he was. The forest was dim, and thick tendrils of mist curled between the trees. The blanket was sodden. David sat up, and a bolt of pain shot through his head. His leg still ached with the same sharp throb. With the pain came memory. The bike. The tree. Bear. Cabal. He looked around, but the clearing was empty. Even the spot where the fire had been had disappeared. Had he dreamed it? But the forest was still there. Bear had abandoned him, then. He'd have to find his own way back to the bike.

He struggled to get to his feet. Putting weight on the leg made him cry out, sharply. It felt as though it was broken. And his head felt worse than it had the night before. Much worse.

"Will you return my cloak now, David Baird? Or were you planning to steal that too?"

He turned to find Bear holding a clay pot of water in one hand and a small loaf in the other. He held both out to David. "Break your fast," he said simply. "Then we'll look for your motor . . . cycle, is it?" Then, as David swayed on his feet, Bear added, "Here! Don't faint on me again!" He helped David over to a mossy log at the side of the clearing.

Handing over the blanket, David set to work on the bread, which was chewy and grainy and tasted of smoke. The water was ice cold, with a tang of bracken. "When I saw the campsite gone I thought you'd taken off and left me," he mumbled between mouthfuls. Then he added, "Guess I couldn't have blamed you if you had. You didn't exactly ask for my company."

Bear slung the blanket about him, pinning it on one shoulder with a massive brooch. "It's wise to leave the wood as you found it," he said. "The trees like it. And it leaves no clue for enemies who might be looking for you."

The trees like it? This Bear really must be some kind of loony, David thought. Yet, for some reason, he trusted him. Perhaps it was the level glance of his hazel-brown eyes. Or the hint of laughter in their depths. Even his ridiculous name seemed to suit him somehow, brown and hardy as he was.

"Your head still pains you?" Bear asked.

David nodded. "And my leg even worse."

Bear looked puzzled. "Let me have another look at you, then," he said. As his fingers probed his head and leg, David couldn't help groaning. "So," said Bear. "Still no signs of an injury. But you're clearly hurting. Are you dizzy?"

David nodded, then wished he hadn't. It felt as if the top of his head were going to fall off!

"The blacks of your eyes are like pinpoints," Bear went on, peering at him intently. "So there's something badly wrong. I'm no healer, but I know the signs. You'll have to lie up somewhere for a while. Head injuries can be dangerous. I've seen it after a battle."

Battle? David shivered. "I . . . I want to go home," he said unsteadily. Then hated himself for whining like a little kid. "Let's find my motorcycle," he added. "If it's working, you could help me get it on the road." Though he couldn't help wondering how he could ride it with his leg the way it was.

Bear looked surprised. "There's no road here," he said. "Only the old track through the forest. But let's go and look. Lean on me."

With Bear supporting David, they set off in the direction he had come from. It was a painful journey, but at last they reached the glade where he had awakened. As Bear had said, there was no road, only a narrow track through a gap in the trees. And the motorcycle was nowhere to be seen.

"It has to be here, it has to!" David cried, breaking away from Bear and stumbling into the glade.

Bear stood watching him for a moment, then he paced back and forth across the glade, his eyes on the ground. "Nothing," he said at last, looking back at David. "A few animal tracks, old ones. The moss torn up here, where you must have scrabbled around, and some bushes broken where you blundered through. That's all."

"But it must be here!" David said wildly. " I was riding the bike down a road, see. And a tree—that one, over there, I think—just appeared out of nowhere. And I hit it. I was knocked out. When I woke up, I couldn't find the bike in the dark. You believe me, don't you? I swear it's the truth!"

Bear met his eyes for a long moment. Then, "You'd better sit down," he said, helping him over to a flat rock at the edge of the glade. "I believe you're telling me the truth—at least what you think is the truth. Though what it means, I don't know. Let me look about. Cabal, stay." He drew his sword and disappeared among the trees.

David sank down on the rock, holding his throbbing head in both hands. The great wolfhound sat watching him, his tail brushing back and forth on the ground ever so slightly.

After some minutes, Bear returned. "It's no use," he said, looking down at David. "There's no sign of anything unusual. No one but you has been here. I could tell if someone had been, from tracks and other signs. So no one could have come and taken this thing of yours. And you said you couldn't find it last night. It's as if it were never here at all."

David gazed up at him numbly. "I don't know what to do," he said. "I don't know where I am, or how to get back to Caerleon. That's where my father is. Do you know the way, Bear?"

Bear shook his head. "It's a place I don't know. But come. You're hurt somehow, though I can't find the cause of it. You need care. We'll go back to my village. There'll be help for your hurts there, and mayhap someone will have heard of Caerleon. But it's more than a day away. Can you walk that far if I help you?"

David shook his head, numbly. "I...I don't think so. My leg hurts pretty badly."

Bear frowned, considering. "Yet there's no other choice. I can't leave you here, and it's too far to bring help quickly. If only I'd brought a boat up the Usk. It would be shorter that way!" He shook his head, "Well, no use bemoaning what can't be changed. Perhaps splints on the leg will help, though there seems to be no break in it."

Turning away, he took out his dagger and cut some rough splints from a sapling. These he bound to his patient's leg using strips of cloth cut from David's jeans. Another sapling provided a rough crutch.

"It's the best I can do, lad," he said, as David pulled himself painfully to his feet. "I fear you've a bad time ahead of you."

David gritted his teeth, and took a few steps. The crutch helped, but not a lot.

Before they left the glade, Bear went over to the giant oak. "Tell me, Old One," he said, placing his palm flat against the trunk. He stood for a few moments, as though listening to something far off, then he patted the rough bark. "My thanks," he said softly. "Bide well."

David watched, numbly. Bad enough to be lost in the middle of a forest that shouldn't even be there. But with a guy who talked to the trees? He didn't want to think about it.

The journey to the village took them two days. For David, it was a walking nightmare. Part of it passed in a kind of sick dream. At other times, as though from far away, he heard himself yelling at Bear, telling him to leave him alone, let him rest, sleep. And trying to fight him when he was forced to go on. At night, he fell into heavy sleep, only to awake, shivering, with the terrible pain in his head and leg.

It began to rain, and the damp added to his misery. The throb of his leg was a dull agony. As if that weren't enough, his head seemed to be getting worse, and his vision had begun to blur. But somehow he stumbled on, one arm around Bear's shoulders. By the end of the second day he was only half-conscious.

He smelled the village before his blurred vision could make it out. The reek of it was like a blow to his nose after the moist green scent of the forest, and it roused him part-way from his stupor. The ripe smell of wood smoke, dressed hides and dung almost made him retch. When he could make out what lay before him, he gaped in amazement. This was not the trim stone village he'd been expecting. It looked to be no more than a dripping huddle of huts in a clearing by a river. He winced as a wave of shouting children and barking dogs bore down on them.

"You're early back, Bear!"

"Have you caught a Saxon? Can I stick him with my spear?"

"Quiet, the pack of you!" roared Bear. "Does he look like a Saxon? What's the matter with your eyes? More like he's of the Fair Folk and will ill-wish you for your rudeness!"

The clamour stopped abruptly, and the children fell back to a respectful distance.

"Is Emrys to house, Arianrod?" Bear demanded of a bold-faced little girl who had dared to stay closer than the rest. She nodded. "And we'll need Branwyn. Fetch her there. Be quick!" She spun on her heel and raced off.

As they passed through the village, men looked up, frowning, from their tasks. Women came to the doors of the huts, then called their children and pulled them inside. At last they came to a hut on the far edge of the village. Bear stopped outside the door. "Myrddin Emrys," he called. "I bring a sick stranger to your door. May we enter?"

"Enter, and be welcome," said a deep voice.

Lifting the door-flap, Bear pushed David inside, motioning him to a bed-box that held a pile of furs. Too weary to wonder or protest, David stumbled over and sank down on them.

A tall man with a long beard streaked with grey got up from a chair. "You've returned," he said to Bear. "It's high time. But what coil is this?"

"I fear it's the Lady," Bear replied.

Emrys' shaggy brows drew together.

"He's bad hurt, Emrys," Bear hurried on. "I know he is, though I can find no actual injury. It's as if he's had a wicked blow to the head, and his leg pains him as if it's broken. He's dizzy, sick. His vision must be blurred, for he keeps walking into things if I let go of him. It's been two days now, and I've had to drag him every step of the way, ranting and raving. I knew he shouldn't be moved, but what else could I do? I couldn't leave him there for the beasts of Forest Fawr to make a meal of."

"Have you sent for Branwyn? I'll need her skills." Emrys knelt down beside David, placing his hand on his forehead. David stared up into his deep black eyes for a moment, then closed his own. The man's hand felt cool and dry on his burning skin. David let himself slip away into blessed darkness.

THREE

There's a . . . strangeness about it, Emrys. I could feel it in the Old One. I touched it as you've taught me. Asked it what was amiss. I could get no clear answer, but something had happened that disturbed it. Deeply. It felt like ripples spreading in a pool. And the Lady was there. And she followed us."

"Didn't he tell you what happened?"

"He tried to, but he didn't make much sense. He's been delirious most of the way, babbling about his father. And someone named Jamie. There's a darkness in him—I don't know how else to put it. He's been in some sort of bad trouble, I think. Quarrelled with his father as well."

"Kin-wrecked? Perhaps that's what drew the Lady to him."

A woman's voice. "And what of his hurts? Bear was right—I can find no wound on his head, and his leg's not broken. Yet he's in terrible pain, and feverish with it."

The voices seemed to be coming from far away. David felt as if he were swimming up from dark depths toward a distant light. But it was still too much effort to reach the surface, and he sank again into sleep.

Much later, he felt something cool on his face and opened his eyes wearily. Very close above him was a face. A clear oval face, framed in a cloud of soot-black hair. Dark-blue eyes looked down into his, and a voice said, "Sleep, David Baird, I didn't mean to wake you."

How could she know my name when I don't know hers? he wondered as he slid under the surface again. Maybe angels don't have names.

It seemed that only minutes passed before someone raised his head and put a bowl of something sharp-smelling to his lips. He swallowed a draught that tasted of bitter herbs. Choked. Then, "Is it the angel again?" he gasped.

"Angel? Whatever's that?" said a merry voice. David opened his eyes. A buxom woman with a great coil of greying braids piled on the top of her head was kneeling at his side, holding a bowl. When she saw his startled expression, she sat back on her heels, grinning. "I'm not the one you were expecting, I see," she said. "Well, aren't you the lad, then. Scarcely back from the gates of Annuvin, and already after the women!"

David sat up, wincing as pain shot through his leg. Then he realized he was stark naked under the rough blanket and pulled it up to his shoulders, blushing. His head still hurt too, though not as much as before. "I . . . I . . . Excuse me, lady. I thought you were the other one."

She chuckled. "Lady me no ladies. My name is plain Branwyn to all. As to that other one, I think I'd better have the care of you from now on. Too much excitement isn't good for a fever, my lad."

A shadow fell across them from the door-place. "So you're back among us, David Baird! And keeping Branwyn amused too. What's the joke?" It was Bear with Cabal behind him.

David shot Branwyn an embarrassed glance.

She winked. "Aye, and he seems a likely lad enough, now he's back in his senses," she said cheerfully. "Now I've others to tend to," she said, turning back to David. "I want you to lie here and let my draught do you good. Don't you dare try to get up yet!" She patted him on the shoulder, then got up and bustled out.

"How long have I been sick?" asked David.

"Nearly a week."

"You're kidding!"

"You mean . . . jesting? No."

David looked around at the hut, remembering how he came to be there. He shivered.

"Don't look so glum. You're alive, after all!" said Bear.

"Sorry," said David. "It's just . . ."

"It's just that nothing's right, is it? And you hoped it would be."

"Something like that," David admitted.

"Take my advice. Get better before you brood overmuch on it." Bear handed David a rough tunic and helped him pull it over his head, tucking the blanket round him again. "Now drink this broth Branwyn has left for you," he added, holding out a bowl. "After you've sat up for a day, we'll think of getting you on your feet. Rest now."

Left alone, David felt black panic rising in him. What had happened to him? His head throbbed. He took a deep breath, then let it go. Bear's right, he told himself. If I think of it all now, I'll go mad. So I won't. Not yet.

He settled back against the cushions and looked about him. The hut was built of rough planks, with a thatched roof and a floor of beaten earth. Embers smouldered in a stone-edged fire pit in the centre of the hut. Above it hung a large iron cauldron, which was suspended by chains from a cross-beam. Smoke from the fire eddied up lazily through a hole in the roof. The furniture was simple—a pair of wooden stools, and the carved chair Emrys had sat in. Two large wooden chests were pushed against the wall, and an odd-shaped object muffled in a heavy cloth stood beside the chair.

Must be some kind of crazy back-to-nature commune, David decided. Home-made granola and bean curd. Weave your own clothes. Build your own hut. Though he'd never heard of such things in Wales. Still, back here in the hills . . .

He tried to drift off to sleep again, but couldn't. For a while he amused himself by trying to identify the sounds he could make out. Voices of people passing near the hut. The barking of dogs and the distant lowing of cattle. Shrieks of children at play. A rhythmic chink-clink that he couldn't identify. Bird song from the forest round about. And woven through it all, the voice of the river running.

The square of dusty sunlight in the door-place shifted across the floor. It must be hours since anyone had come. If only he could get up and look outside. But Branwyn had said not to. His restless glance kept returning to the object by Emrys's chair. It was the only unusual thing in the room, and somehow it drew him. He pushed back the blanket and tried to get up, but his leg gave an agonizing twinge, and his head swam. Still determined to have a look, he rolled on his side. By reaching out and stretching, he managed to tug the cloth away.

Underneath was a harp. Small, less than three feet tall, it was made of some golden-glowing wood. It was sweetly curved on one side, straight on the other. He simply had to hold it. Though his injured leg gave another warning twinge, he swung his good leg over the side of the bed-box and managed to reach the harp and drag it back to the bed-box. He sat holding it on his lap, his pains forgotten. The harp rested securely, as if it belonged there.

"Oh, you beauty!" whispered David, drawing his fingers lightly across it. Just the quiver of the strings under his fingertips made him tremble with pleasure. The harp answered his touch with a few silvery notes, almost like a question.

"No, I don't know how to play you," he said. There seemed to be no way to tune the harp. At first, he plucked the strings at random, just getting the feel. Then he began trying to pick out one of his own songs, a slow one. The melody was easy enough, but getting the harmony was harder. It was different from the guitar. But not impossibly different, he told himself. After a while, not noticing, he began to sing softly along with the notes.

"Your voice is true. Though the song is strange to the ear." Emrys stood in the door-place, leaning on a stout wooden staff.

David stopped singing, but made no movement to give up the harp. "I hope you don't mind," he said. "Once I found what it was, I just had to."

Emrys sniffed. "You don't play well. But not too badly."

"Harp's not my instrument. I was just trying to figure it out."

Emrys's bushy eyebrows rose. "You've never harped before?"

David shook his head. "I play acoustic guitar, mostly. He shrugged. "It's not hard to pick up more instruments, though. In the band I can play a set on just about anything. Percussion, bass, keyboard synthesizer. I sing lead, too."

"I know not these strange instruments." Emrys sat down heavily in his chair and stared at David. "Are you claiming to be a bard?" he asked, frowning.

"A . . ? No, I don't think so. What is it?"

"A minstrel. A singer and a player of instruments. One who knows the music and traditions of his people, and acts as their memory. And their inspiration."

"Memory? Inspiration?" David was puzzled. "No, I'm nothing like that. I'm just a guy who makes music. I'm not much on tradition. I make up my own songs."

"A bard does that, too." There was a long silence, then Emrys said, "That strange song you were singing. Is it yours?"

David nodded.

"Play it for me again. If it will not tire you."

David grinned. "Music always makes me feel better," he said. He bent over the harp and began to play. This time, he stumbled less. He tried to weave more complex harmonies, as he would have done on the guitar, though only some of it worked. He ran through the tune twice, then swung into the vocal.

There was a silence when he finished. At last, Emrys said, "Your music is not as ours is. But you are gifted. You must be, to get even this far so quickly."

"Your harp makes it easy. It's a lovely thing. If it were mine, I'd call it . . . Beauty," said David, half embarrassed.

Emrys's eyebrows shot up again. "As it happens, that is its name," he said. "Though how you came to know it, I can't guess. A harp's true name is a secret known only to its master."

Feeling awkward, David said, "Would you play something for me? I'd like to hear what Beauty should really sound like."

Emrys reached over and took the harp. He settled it on his knee. Then he took from around his neck an object threaded on a cord. It looked something like an old-fashioned roller-skate key. He applied this to the tuning screws of the harp, pausing now and again to pluck the strings and listen. At last, satisfied with the tuning, he put the key away. After a moment's thought, he struck a fierce chord and began to sing in a rich, clear voice.

> *Black flew the ravens in their fatal flight,*
> *Dark the woods, dark the night . . .*

A prickle of excitement ran down David's spine. The music was like nothing he had ever heard before.

Passionate, strange, its cadences wound around him and drew him in. And the words, too, pulled him in, made him live them. The wild ride of a doomed band of heroes. The desperate fight against impossible odds. The bloody battlefield where all but honour was lost.

> *Cruel their fell fate, yet their courage a star.*
> *So perished the heroes of lost Trenovar.*

So rapt was David that for a moment he didn't realize that the song had ended. He came to himself with a shiver, his eyes brimming. Embarrassed, he quickly blinked the tears back.

He drew a deep breath and said, "That was, that was... I've never heard anything like it. It's wonderful!"

Emrys sat in the gathering dusk, the harp cradled on his lap. David had the uncomfortable feeling that the man knew quite well that he had been moved to tears.

At last Emrys said, "Would you like me to teach you something of our music?"

To have a chance to learn to play Beauty as it should be played?

"Would I!" said David. Though to himself he added, But I won't be staying here all that long!

FOUR

The next day, Branwyn said David could get up. "But go no farther than the bench outside the door, mind," she scolded. "Help him get dressed, Bear. There are clean trews and tunic laid ready for him."

"What am I, a nursemaid?" growled Bear. But he obeyed, handing David his crutch once he was dressed.

Outside, David was glad enough to sink down on the bench. Though his head felt much better, his leg still hurt fiercely.

Wincing at the brightness, he shaded his eyes and looked around. The village was larger than he had thought. But there was still something utterly wrong about it. His heart sank.

Bear watched him narrowly. "Feeling strange? Sit you here awhile. I must go to arms training. Old Rufus will flay me if I'm late again!" Bear seized a handful of broad-bladed spears and an oval shield that stood leaning against the side of the hut, and bounded off down the path, Cabal loping easily at his heels.

David sat a long time, gazing numbly at the river. One of the village girls glanced at him shyly as she swung by on her way to get water. She was wearing a long belted tunic down to the ground, with a cloak pinned at the shoulder with a brooch, as Bear's was. Her russet hair, braided in three long plaits, was trimmed with gleaming golden balls.

She made a pretty picture as she stooped to dip her water jug into the river. Yet the sight of her suddenly focussed his fear as a lens focusses light. The way these people dressed, lived. Swords. Shields. Spears. Talk of battles. Though the sun was still warm upon him, he felt deadly cold.

"You're troubled." Emrys was standing behind him in the door-place.

"I'm scared to death," said David shakily. "I look around me and my eyes don't believe what they see."

Emrys sat down beside him, folding his gnarled hands on his staff. "It's time you told me what happened before you met Bear." As David opened his mouth to begin, Emrys added sternly, "And be sure you speak the truth. Hide nothing, or it will be the worse for you."

"Yessir." Haltingly, David told it all, Emrys interrupting him with sharp questions from time to time.

"You saw the owl first, before anything unusual happened?"

David nodded. "It swooped at me a couple of times. Then it lit on a bush and watched me."

"And after that you saw the lights? They were mounting the valley toward the ruins?"

"Yes."

"The *canyll-y-corf*!" muttered Emrys. "And you rode right at them?" His voice hardened. "Why would you do such a thing?"

"I don't know! The idea just popped into my head, I guess," David said. "I was still mad at my dad...oh, at the whole world, I guess. I thought I'd give them a scare. Pretty stupid of me."

"Stupid? It was madness!" snapped the bard. "To challenge the Dark Ones among the hollow hills!"

"I . . . I don't understand."

Emrys snorted. "The *canyll-y-corf* is a procession of the spirits of the Dark Ones, a mourning for their great dead back to the dawn of time. It's a wonder they didn't just destroy you outright, instead of throwing you . . . away." He sighed, then added, half to himself, "I suppose that's her doing. She used their power . . ."

"But where am I? Nothing in your world looks like what I remember!" said David. "It . . . it all looks like some crazy movie set!"

"You're in southwest Prydein, not too far north of the great river Hafren," said Emrys. "This river is the Usk, which flows into Hafren. Beyond those hills behind us is the old Roman road from Isca to Deva."

"I don't know any of those places. Only . . . yes! Something about Isca!" He'd heard that name before. But where? "Have you any maps, Emrys?" he asked. "I mean . . . pictures of the land drawn on paper?"

Emrys snorted. "We aren't savages, boy, whatever you may think of us. Of course we know of maps. But we have none here. The High King and his war leaders in the Land of Summer have many, of course."

David flushed. "Sorry. Could . . . could you sketch me a rough map to show where Isca is?" he asked.

"I could," returned Emrys. "But better yet, here's Bear. Let him try. We'll soon see if he remembers my teaching as well as he does Rufus' cutting and thrusting."

Bear and Cabal had appeared among a group of boys at the end of the village street. Taking leave of them, Bear came slowly on alone. As he got closer, David could see that his tunic was wet with sweat and powdered over with dust.

Emrys looked Bear up and down. "Rufus works you hard, I see. Well, I'm as stern a taskmaster."

"That I've never doubted," said Bear shortly. "I've had as many welts from that staff of yours as from Rufus's cudgel."

"Then show me that you've learned from them," snapped Emrys. "Draw David a map of west Prydein, showing our location here."

Bear groaned. "Born to take orders, I." He stacked his weapons against the hut. Then he unsheathed his sword. With the tip, he drew in the dirt a ragged coastline inset with a great tapering wedge-shape.

"West Prydein," he said. "This V-shape is where the river Hafren becomes one with the sea." Toward the point of the V and a little above it he drew a small X. "Isca. Once a fort of the Romans. There are many ruins, and a few folk dwell near there still," he added. Then he moved the point of the sword and drew a line down to join the Hafren. Beside it he drew another X. "The river Usk. The village. About two days' journey afoot from Isca. Much less by river." He looked quizzically at David, who was staring down at the crude map.

For a moment, David couldn't figure it out. Then suddenly it made sense. "The river you call Hafren—it must be the Severn!" he said, with growing excitement. "The wide part opening to the sea is the Bristol Channel. And Isca. North of the river, but not far away . . . Isca could be Caerleon! The place I came from that night."

He stared at the map, his excitement growing. "It would fit," he went on. "The road I followed on the bike went north, roughly. Then there was a crossroads, and I turned west a bit, and climbed up into the hills. I must have been quite far north and west when the . . . accident happened. And then Bear brought me here. That's back to the east, isn't it? Two days' journey."

Bear nodded.

"Isca is the same place as Caerleon," David said. "It has to be. But why do you call it by a different name? And why are things so different from what I'm used to? Places, clothes—everything! Is it just here, in these woods and this village that it's so?"

Emrys shook his head. "Branwyn and I have never seen anything like the clothing you wore. And the strange machine you told me about, the one you rode upon—these things are not part of our world. Not anywhere that I have ever heard of, in Prydein or across the seas."

"But what does it all mean?" cried David. "I'm not far from where I'm supposed to be. But everything is wrong! Or have I gone crazy?" His head began to throb, and he hid his face in his hands. Cabal whined, and laid his head beside David's knee.

There was a long silence. At last David raised his

head, and looked from one to the other of them. "What date is it? I mean, what year?" His mouth felt dry as he asked the question.

"I don't know what reckoning you use," said Emrys. "We British reckon it as the twentieth year of the reign of our High King. "The Romans had a different reckoning, however. As do the Saxons now."

"That's no help, then," said David impatiently. After a moment he added, "Then it all comes back to Isca and Caerleon. That's the only thing I'm sure of. You say Isca belonged to the Romans. But that was ages ago!"

"Nay, they left Prydein only in my great-grandsire's time," said Emrys. "They were an army from across the sea. Their emperors conquered Prydein, destroying many of our tribes. They built Isca and other cities. And a network of roads to move their armies."

He paused, reflecting. "Many of our folk came to believe Roman ways were better than our own. They lived in Roman towns, learned the Latin language. Only a few, our clan among them, kept to the wild hills and lived in the old ways. Then, after hundreds of years, enemies besieged Rome. The Romans sailed away and left those who had trusted them to the mercy of the Saxons." He spat in the dust.

David's mind raced. Romans had crucified Jesus, hadn't they? That was hundreds and hundreds of years ago. Thousands! But Emrys had said the Romans were in Prydein in his great-grandfather's time!

"The answer has been staring me in the face all along," he said at last. "Except I won't believe it. Can't. My problem isn't *where* I am, it's *when* I am!"

"What?" asked Bear, puzzled.

"I'm not far from Caerleon, where I started from," said David despairingly. "But I'm nearly two thousand years back in time!"

That evening they sat late around the fire in the hut. David was sunk in silence, his bowl of stew untouched before him. Emrys and Bear spoke together in low voices, glancing at him from time to time.

At last he raised his head and looked at the two of them accusingly. "Why don't you tell me I'm wrong, that it's impossible?" he asked. "Then I'd only have to worry about being crazy!"

Emrys leaned back in his chair. "Impossible? Who knows what's possible?" he said. "Many wise folk believe that time isn't a road we travel and leave behind us. They say past and present and future run side by side, with the thinnest of curtains between them. For certes, there are those who can see into the past and future."

"You, for example," Bear put in unexpectedly.

Emrys shrugged. "I have my . . . visions. But I can't foretell the future, no matter what the fools of villagers believe. You know that well enough."

"This is the weirdest conversation I've ever heard," said David. "You mean I've sort of slipped sideways into your time?"

"Possibly," agreed Emrys.

"But we must be speaking some language I've never even heard of," David protested.

Now that he'd thought of it, he knew they were. He'd known all along, with the part of his mind that lived in music. It was a language with an up and down lilt to it that was almost like singing. He frowned, trying to hear exactly how the words they were speaking were different from English words. But the effort made his head swim, and he gave it up. "So, how come I understand what you're saying?" he finished lamely.

Emrys shrugged. "Who can tell?"

Bear stood up and stretched, yawning hugely. "It'll do no good to pother on about this all night," he said. "Either you're here or you're not. And it looks to me as if you are." He gave David a considering look. "I, for one, am glad. Emrys is always trying to knock some education into my thick head. But just think what's locked up inside that noggin of yours!"

"You'll have to think of more than that," said Emrys. "David must learn to live here, at least for now. He'll share the hut with you and me. After all, where else can he stay? I'll make a start at teaching him harping, but you must teach him the rest. In a few weeks, once he's well enough, get Rufus to show him how to defend himself. Tell him I ask it as a favour." He turned to David and added, "Though I can see from your frame you're no warrior."

Warrior! "It . . . it isn't the thing to be where I come from," said David.

"However, you may have the makings of a minstrel," Emrys went on, "and it will be my business to instruct you in that."

David swallowed hard. "You mean I just settle down and try to get along here? Aren't you going to do anything? Send me back to my own time?"

"How do you propose I do that?" asked Emrys dryly.

"Well . . . I don't know," floundered David. "Don't you?"

"Not in the least," said Emrys.

FIVE

Soft spring stars hung so close above the forest that they seemed tangled in the topmost branches of the trees. David drew a deep breath of damp air as he and Emrys made their way toward the light and noise of the chieftain's hall at the other end of the village.

Five long, puzzling weeks had passed. David had quickly learned the rudiments of harping, and Emrys had taught him a number of songs. David had soon found out that Emrys was the toughest teacher he had ever had. He accepted absolutely no excuse for mistakes. And, though Emrys had never used his staff on David the way Bear claimed he did on him, there were moments that he looked as if he'd like to.

Time after time, David had been on the point of rebelling. Only the fierceness of Emrys' gaze, and David's awareness of how much he owed to Emrys and Bear made him bite his tongue and struggle on.

Aside from his harping, David had found himself lonely. Bear was away from the hut much of the time, either training with the other youths or hunting. Like Emrys, he also spent long hours in the chieftain's hall. Left to himself, David wondered more and more about the two of them. Emrys didn't seem to be Bear's father. At least, Bear never called him father. But if that was so, where was Bear's family? Sometimes it was on the tip of David's tongue to ask, but despite Bear's friendliness, there was something closed about him, as if he were hiding a great hurt. David shrank from pestering him with questions.

At first, the pain in David's head and leg discouraged him from exploring the village. Gradually, though, he began to feel better. Almost, he told himself, puzzled, as if his invisible wounds were healing.

He began limping about a bit, hoping to find someone to talk to, but people glanced at him suspiciously, as if wondering what he was doing among them. So he'd ended by brooding alone in the hut for many hours each day, with only Beauty to keep him company.

Then, a week before, Emrys had disappeared without a word of explanation. After a few days, tired of going over the same old lessons, David had asked Bear when Emrys would be back. Bear had just shrugged.

"Who knows? Oft times he journeys between the tribes, on business known only to himself, or perhaps the High King. Other times he wanders in the woods with moss in his hair and bark in his beard. He only half likes being around people anyway. Sometimes I think he'd rather live in the woods with just the animals to hear his harping." Bear had grinned. "Emrys Wyllt, people call him behind his back. Wild Emrys." Then his expression changed. "But to me he's always been true Emrys," he had added soberly. "He took me in, orphan stray that I am, and I'm not forgetting that, harsh taskmaster though he sometimes is."

So Bear had no family of his own, David thought. That went a long way toward explaining the separateness that he wore about him like a cloak, though clearly he was well liked by all in the village.

Despite Bear's words, David was still startled when Emrys suddenly turned up that evening looking worn and travel-stained. He had scarcely taken time to wash and change his tunic before he picked up Beauty and slung it over his back.

"Come. We're summoned by Lord Rhodri," he said to David.

"Huh? What for?"

"It's time," was all Emrys would say. The bard did not seem worried, but David was. He'd only seen the chieftain from a distance, but given his size and the length of his sword, he felt that was close enough.

An owl hooted close by in the woods. David shivered.

Emrys glanced at him. "Fate is a gift both bright and dark," he said. "The wise accept it whole. Perhaps you are wrong to fear the owl so."

That's a lot of help! thought David. If it weren't for that blasted owl I wouldn't be stuck here.

They crossed the beaten earth of the exercise ground. At the doors of the hall, two tall warriors clashed their spears across the doorway.

"Emrys, harper to Rhodri Mawr," said the bard formally. "And the stranger. We are summoned."

The spears clashed back, and they stepped into the smoky hall. It was a rectangular building, by far the largest in the village. Huge fire pits blazed at each end, and over them cauldrons bubbled and roasting carcasses turned on spits. The air was rich with the savoury smell of meat. In cubicles along the sides of the hall, warriors and their followers sat on benches feasting and drinking.

Rhodri and his council sat around a plank table on a dais at the far end of the hall. They were big men with fierce drooping moustaches, dressed richly in bright-patterned trews and tunics woven of coloured cloth with embroidered borders. Gold gleamed everywhere about them—on thick twisted torcs around their necks, on the massive brooches that pinned their cloaks, in bracelets and armbands on their sinewy arms, on the gemmed hilts of their swords and daggers. Gold and silver too were the goblets and the gaming board set out on the table. After the brown drabness of the village, it was dazzling.

Rhodri looked down frowning as Emrys and David came up. Seen up close he was bigger, broader, and even more impressive than from a distance, though his fox-red hair was well threaded with silver. "It's long since you've bothered to grace my hall, Emrys," he growled. "A lord shouldn't have to summon his harper."

"My regrets, Rhodri son of Pwyll," Emrys replied courteously. "As you know, my calling often takes me to distant places. I must serve more needs than your own. And lately, I've had the care of this stranger."

"That's another quarrel between us," returned the chieftain, still frowning. "Who is he, and why is he living in the village after so many weeks? Why hasn't he returned to his own people by now?"

If only I could! thought David. Glancing around

nervously he noticed Bear standing with some other young warriors. He looked grim, and David's heart sank.

"He cannot return home yet, my lord," said Emrys. "Bear found him wandering and injured. He comes from . . . across the Western Sea."

"Western Sea? He's not one of the cursed Scoti, is he?" asked Rhodri suspiciously. "I'd as soon shelter a viper under my cloak as aid one of them! They're almost as bad as the Saxons, those plundering devils."

A low growl of agreement ran around the hall.

"Nay, my lord. His home is farther west even than that. Perhaps almost as far as the Fortunate Isles."

Rhodri stroked his shaggy moustache. "Well, he's not the first stray you've brought me," he said at last. At these words, Bear stepped forward grinning and bowed deeply.

Rhodri nodded to him. "Aye, lad, you've worked out well enough. But this one's different. From the looks of him, he'll never make a warrior. And we can't afford to feed useless mouths." Rhodri threw himself back in his chair, his eyes narrowed to slits of blue ice. "I see no reason to keep this scrawny youngster. Unless we make a drudge of him."

A drudge! David froze in horror. He'd noticed a few miserable creatures doing the dirtiest work of the village, and felt pity for them. Would that be his fate?

"Nay, Rhodri Mawr!" cried Emrys in a ringing voice. "Would you enslave a nightingale? Set a lark to swilling the swine?"

"What mean you, bard?" Rhodri was scowling again.

"Only that you have here before you a harper of

possible talent. He has studied with me only a little, but already . . . Nay, hear for yourself. I'll stand by your judgement."

A long moment passed. Then, "See that you do," said Rhodri grimly.

Emrys unslung Beauty from his back and snapped his fingers. A servant scurried forward with a low stool, and placed it before him. Emrys held out the harp to David. "Give them *Culhwych and Olwen*," he said in a low voice. "It always goes over well." Then, noting David's panicky expression, he added, "They're a sentimental lot, though they don't look it. Just follow my setting."

David took the harp, his heart beating wildly. He settled himself on the stool and began tuning Beauty, grateful for a few moments in which to regain his wits.

At Rhodri's command, warriors gathered slowly from the far corners of the hall.

David looked down at the harp. Beauty, be with me now, he thought in panic, clutching its warm wood.

Taking a deep breath, he struck a chord into the silence. For one dreadful moment he couldn't remember what followed. Then, as if of their own will, his fingers sought out the melody, drilled into him by Emrys. Once through, and then he began to sing.

When Culhwych fell first in love with Olwen fair . . .

Little by little, the magic of the song took him. The hopeless love of the hero for Olwen the Fair. The terrible ordeals he had to overcome to win her wicked father's consent to their marriage. The faith of her love for him through all.

At first, he played as Emrys had taught him. Then, caught in web of his own spinning, he modulated the key and the song turned stranger and wilder. At last, with the final verse, he returned to the major key, with its sound of great gladness.

And they were wed, and in rare happiness ran their days.

He swept one last chord, then laid his hand on Beauty's strings to still them. And came back to himself.

There was silence in the hall, followed by the buzz of many voices. David got awkwardly to his feet.

"Impertinent puppy! You took a dreadful chance. You couldn't just play it the way I taught you, could you?" Emrys growled in his ear. Then, turning away and raising his voice he cried, "Rhodri Mawr, what say you now?"

"I say . . ." Rhodri glared under his eyebrows around the table and then out across the hall, daring anyone else to speak. Then he smacked the flat of his hand on the table so hard that the goblets danced. "I say you spoke the truth, Emrys. The young pup has something of the minstrel about him. Though he plays strangely enough. I say he deserves his chance. Now, what say the rest of you?"

A hum of approval went round the hall. One old warrior reeled up and slapped David on the back, offering him a draught of rank-smelling ale.

His knees still trembling, David nearly collapsed.

SIX

N ow," said Emrys, "you start to work."
"Start! What do you call what I've been doing all these weeks?" David was indignant.

Emrys snorted. Bear, who was tossing scraps to Cabal, laughed out loud.

"Don't let a little praise last night turn your head," said Emrys. "You've made a beginning, no more. Your fingering is atrocious. You know no more than a ballad or two. What possible use do you think you'll be to me or the clan?"

"Use?"

"Use. D'you think being a minstrel is no more than spinning some song you happen to think of?" Emrys wagged a forefinger under David's nose. "That may be so in that strange future world you say you belong to. Here it's different!"

"Different how?"

"A bard has a responsibility. How much I can teach you, I don't know. You're not one of us, for one thing. And you're old, for another. True bards are trained from childhood up. But I've vouched for you to Rhodri Mawr, and I intend to see to it that you learn what you need to know to be useful to me. And to him."

Great! David thought. He's just like my dad. Always wanting me to do stuff his way. "What am I, some kind of slave?" he mumbled.

Emrys shrugged. "A slave to music? Yes, if that's what it takes to train you." He narrowed his eyes. "Of course, if you'd rather swill the swine . . ." he added.

"Thanks, but no thanks!" said David.

But it wasn't long before he began to think that pigs might have their charms after all. David spent hour after hour on fingering, chords, harmony. Then, when his fingers cracked and bled, more hours studying ballads, songs, stories, chants, histories of clans and tribes, the genealogies of kings and chieftains. All of it had to be memorized. Word perfect.

"Like being a walking data bank," he grumbled. But he took care that Emrys didn't hear.

And his troubles had barely started.

He'd got used to seeing Bear only at mealtimes, or when he sat mumbling to himself trying to master one of Emrys's lessons. Then, one afternoon, Emrys released David early.

"I'm going up-river and will be away for some time again. Go on with what we've been doing. I'll expect improvement when you play it for me again," he said curtly. "Don't disappoint me."

David nodded, but the moment Emrys left the hut he threw himself down on the bed-box for a nap.

A none-too-gentle prod in the ribs snapped his eyelids open. "Whaaa? Hey, watch it!" he protested, batting away the butt end of Bear's spear.

"Up," said Bear briefly. "Let's get on with it."

David didn't budge. "On with what?" he snapped. "Emrys has been pounding away at me all day. My brain feels like mush."

Bear grinned mirthlessly. "Welcome to my world," he said. "He teaches me too, don't forget. But Emrys can't teach you everything you need to know. You've got to learn weapons. Remember, Emrys said so."

"Oh, come on," David groaned.

"Up," Bear repeated, prodding him again. "You're fit enough now, that's certain. I haven't seen you limp in weeks."

Still protesting, David swung his feet to the floor. "What do I need to learn weapons for? I'm supposed to become a bard, aren't I? Lord Rhodri himself said I'd never make a warrior."

"I suppose you want to stay alive, though," Bear returned coolly. "D'you expect the rest of us to wet-nurse you? Cudgel and spear and dagger you'll learn. Enough so you can take a wee walk in the woods without getting yourself killed."

Bear chose two cudgels from the rack near the door and picked up a breast-plate made of boiled leather like his own. "There's a clearing in the woods we can use," he said, jerking his thumb over his shoulder. "No use taking you to the practice ground—yet."

David followed him, muttering under his breath. Who did Bear think he was, anyway?

When they reached the clearing, Bear unbuckled his sword and laid it aside. He hefted a cudgel in one hand. "Hold it so—hands well apart, nearer one end than the other," he said. "Feet well apart, too. Knees bent just a bit. For balance, that is." He tossed the cudgel to David.

David staggered as he caught it. It was much heavier than it looked, and he could barely hold it level with both hands. There was nearly six feet of it, all solid wood. After a few minutes of feinting according to Bear's instructions, David's wrists ached and the muscles in his forearms burned.

"Now, I'll thrust at you this way. And you must try and block me. We'll go slowly at first. This way. Now, that way. No, turn as you parry. Are your feet rooted to the ground? It's a kind of dance, man. You have to get the feel of it."

On and on they went, Bear demonstrating the moves, then directing the sequences.

"I'll go for your legs now. Move, can't you? Or I'll have them out from under you!"

Thrust, parry, sweep, with Bear slowly increasing the pace.

David struggled on, panting. Then, "Enough, Bear!" he gasped, stopping dead in his tracks.

Caught off guard, Bear wrenched himself aside to keep from hitting David. His cudgel whizzed through the air just inches from David's left ear.

"Are you daft? Or do you just want to die untimely?" he growled. "Never do such a stupid thing again. I'll say when we stop. Otherwise you'll end up with a cracked crown again. And this time it'll do for you."

"But I . . . can't," gasped David, leaning on his cudgel. "I just can't do it!"

Bear's eyes narrowed. "Oh, yes, you can," he said

coldly, "and you will, because you must. So stop whining, and let's get on with it!"

He aimed a great sweeping blow at David, who jumped back and parried it clumsily.

You stinker! David thought grimly. He struggled on, muscles protesting. Bear's blows seemed to get heavier, and David felt as if his very bones twanged under the assault. A dozen times he wanted to stop again. To convince Bear somehow that enough was enough. Yet the memory of that contemptuous look stung him. Biting down on his anger, he soldiered on.

After a few minutes, Bear stopped to let him catch his breath. Then they went at it again. Another breathing space. And on and on. Only when the sun began to slant toward the edge of the trees did Bear step back and lower his cudgel. David leaned on his, knees trembling with weariness. Bear wasn't even winded. Casting aside his cudgel and pulling off his breastplate, he walked over to a stream at the edge of the clearing. Kneeling, he splashed water over his head and chest, snorting and grunting like his namesake animal. At last he shook himself and stretched out on the mossy bank in a pool of sunlight.

Grudgingly, David followed him. The water was so cold that it burned his sweaty skin. David gasped in surprise, but went on sluicing himself.

"So," said Bear, "tell me about it."

"About what?" said David sullenly.

"Why, the future, of course. Where you come from. What it's like. What people do and why they do it. I don't know why Emrys doesn't talk to you about it. But he's away now, and here's my chance."

David let himself down on the bank and was rewarded with a sharp stab of pain from his tortured muscles. Blast Bear anyway. "Get serious!" he snapped. "You couldn't possibly understand if I did tell you."

Bear's eyes narrowed. "Why not try me? I may not be as stupid as I look."

"I didn't mean . . ." David began. Then he stopped. Because he had, really. He rubbed his sore wrists. What were these people after all but a bunch of dumb primitives? Big muscles and little brains. All of them. Well, except maybe Emrys.

Without another word, Bear got up, collected his breastplate, and strode off across the clearing.

David followed him slowly, his anger ebbing. "Listen," he began as they collected their weapons. "I . . ."

Bear eyed him levelly. "Nay, say no more. I shouldn't have asked you. We've wasted enough time, anyway." He stalked off, leaving David to cope with the cudgels.

All right, if you're going to be so touchy, you big, dumb ox, David thought, resentfully. Well, at least that would be the end of the weapons training.

It wasn't. Bear showed up the next day. He shrugged off David's protests and marched him to the clearing. Again they went at it until David was exhausted. Bear would wait patiently while David caught his breath, only to begin again. And so it went on the day after, and the day after that.

Slowly, David began to improve.

"Yes," Bear would say. "That's something like. Now,

again." To his own surprise, David found himself trying harder. He'd show him!

After three weeks of cudgels, Bear added spears to the workout. More thrust and parry, with the short thrusting spears, with a great heavy shield weighing down David's left arm. Hours and hours of casting the long spears at a straw target.

After a week of this, David was bruised all over and ached in muscles he'd never known he had.

"Well, it's progress of a sort," said Bear, gathering up the spears. "It would take a child two or three minutes to kill you now instead of only one. But as for your marksmanship . . ." He stared at David's spears stuck like a hedge all around the target and shook his head.

He and David pulled them out and stacked them before heading for the stream.

"I never was much good at sports," said David, kneeling beside Bear and wincing as he eased his cramped shoulders out of his breastplate.

"Sports . . . ?" began Bear. Then he fell silent.

"Oh, games—hockey, football," David said after a moment. "The hockey's played on ice. On skates—I mean, sharp blades fastened to boots. To help you slide fast over the ice."

"You mean the ground is covered with ice?" asked Bear after a moment. "All year? How could you stand the cold? How do you grow crops?"

"No, not all year. And not everywhere. Actually, we played hockey in an arena. Oh, lord. An arena is . . ."

"I know what an arena is," said Bear quickly. "The Romans had them. One kind for horse races." A shadow crossed his face. "And another kind for wild-beast fights. And human fights."

"Yeah? We still have places for horse-racing. Not the other. Well, bullfights in Spain, I guess."

And so it began. In the middle, going off in all directions, like a web spun by a crazy spider with no sense of pattern. Day after day, when the training was done they would rest and talk. Sometimes Bear would start it, sometimes David. And the more David told, the more he found himself wanting to tell. To reassure himself that what he remembered was real, that he was who he thought he was.

He often wondered what Bear made of it all. What would he have made of it himself, if he had heard it this way? It couldn't possibly make much sense. But there was a hunger about Bear, a need to know.

"Well, everyone drives cars—I mean, sort of four-wheeled chariots without horses. They burn gas to make them move."

"Gas? Is that like wood?"

"Um, no. Well, sort of, in a way. It's made from plants that died long ago. Oh, longer ago than this. Much longer. Way back in the time of the dinosaurs, I guess."

"Dinosaurs?"

"Oh, lord!"

One day, lying on the bank of the stream, they had begun with the space shuttle and somehow ended with David's father and mother.

On impulse, David glanced at Bear and asked, "What about your folks? Rhodri said Emrys had made him take you in, but . . ."

There was a long silence. Then Bear said slowly, "My mother died in the Saxon wars. In the Land of Summer. That's where Emrys found me. My father . . . " His voice trailed off. Then, "I never had one," he said gruffly.

David was startled. "C'mon, everyone has a father. I mean, you can't get born without one!"

Bear shrugged. "Oh, that. Yes. I guess I should have said my father didn't have a son. Not one he wanted to admit to, anyway."

"You mean your mother and father didn't . . ? Oh, I get it!" said David awkwardly. "Hey, in my time lots of people don't, well, marry. They just live together. They still have children. It doesn't really matter."

"It does here," said Bear soberly. "Who you are depends on your father's clan. Without that, you're an outsider. I never knew who my father was. I suppose my mother was ashamed, and that's why she wouldn't tell me. And now she never can."

"Oh," said David. He didn't know what else to say. Not to even know who you were! His own dad wasn't much of a father, but still . . .

Bear got up quickly. "Come on," he said gruffly. "It's time to get back." He set off so fast that David had to jog to keep up.

SEVEN

The oak cudgel caught David squarely across the ribs with a resounding thwack. Despite his leather armour, the blow knocked the breath out of him. He sank to one knee, gasping, and Cai landed another blow across his shoulders. David landed flat on his face in the dust. The other young warriors standing about guffawed.

"Why do we waste time on this milksop, Rufus?" Cai demanded. The tall, red-headed boy's voice was contemptuous. He prodded David in the ribs with the tip of his cudgel. "He's as weak as a starved cat. And has about as much chance of becoming a warrior!" Cai's followers slapped their knees and laughed uproariously at this sally.

Spitting dirt from between his teeth, David dragged himself wearily to his feet. Gripping his cudgel, he braced himself for another blow. It was his second week at the practice ground with the others, and it wasn't getting any easier. It hadn't taken him long to realize that without Bear's hours of coaching he'd have been far worse off. Bear's strokes seemed gentle compared to the punishment he took from Cai and the others. They seemed to go out of their way to hurt and humiliate him.

"Why do we do it, my fine young lordling?" Rufus asked Cai. "Because Emrys asked me to do it. It's seldom he asks me a favour, and when he does, I think it's wise to do as he asks. I've no desire to wake up one fine morning and find I've been turned into a bat or . . . an owl!"

At this, Cai and his friends stopped laughing. One or two of them thrust out index and little fingers in a gesture to avert evil.

There was an awkward pause. Then Bear, who had been sharpening his dagger on a whetstone, looked up. "Oh, come on, Rufus," he said coolly. "Emrys doesn't turn anybody into anything."

He glanced at David, then at Cai. "Still, I think David's had enough for today," he added. He thrust his dagger into his belt and unsheathed his sword. "Come, Cai. Try a more equal contest," he challenged. A murmur went around the group.

Cai's eyes kindled with an eager blue flame. Tossing the cudgel aside, he picked up his shield and drew his sword. "I admit no equality with you, Bear cub," he said mockingly. "You've never beaten me yet!"

"Oh, but I will, one of these days," said Bear, as the two began to circle one another. "And you know I will." His brown eyes danced.

He actually enjoys this, thought David. He tried not to flinch as the heavy blades sliced through the air and clanged together in thrust and parry. Old Rufus, standing just outside of blade range, looked on, his seamed face intent. "Cai, you ass, you're letting your guard down!" he coached. "Use it, Bear . . . Yes!"

Bear was the faster of the two. Even David could see that. His sword nicked Cai's upper arm, and a thin line of blood welled out of the gash. Cai cursed and redoubled his attack. He was older than Bear, and both taller and heavier. Parrying another thrust, he launched a great, sweeping blow that clove a great wedge out of Bear's wooden shield. Bear parried, and the blades screeched against each other down to their hilts. Cai wrenched free, and another slashing stroke caught Bear off balance. He reeled back, and the tip of Cai's blade grazed his cheek. He gave ground, bleeding.

David took an impulsive step forward, only to find his arm held in an iron grip. "A sword fight is no place for the likes of you," warned Rufus.

"Why do you let them do it? It's not fair! Cai's much bigger and stronger," David said angrily.

Rufus raised his eyebrows. "Do you think our enemies care about a fair fight?" he asked. "A warrior must do what he can. Against any odds. Cai and Bear will fight until one of them yields."

"But Cai might kill him!"

Rufus shook his head. "We don't kill each other in practice. Though Cai may punish Bear badly. But he never has, because Bear fights with his head as much as with his sword."

"You mean he's good? Better than Cai?"

"He hasn't his full height and strength yet. But when he does, he'll be . . . unbeatable." Rufus's face showed the merest trace of a smile.

Long minutes passed, and the swordsmen began to tire. Sweat-stained and covered in dust they circled, looking for an opening. Then Bear found one. Slipping under Cai's guard, his sword slashed wickedly upward, slicing through Cai's leather jerkin. Blood oozed out, and as Cai stumbled and fell to one knee, Bear was on him, his sword at his throat.

"Yield, foster-brother," he said silkily. His voice still sounded amused, but there was an edge to it.

"Of course he yields," said Rufus, stepping between the two and forcing up Bear's blade with the tip of his own. "Cai, you fought like a fool. Fools don't live long in battle. Bear, you were lucky. No, don't scowl at me. You did well, but you made mistakes Cai should have used to finish you."

Bear shrugged. He sheathed his sword. Then he held out his hand and grasped Cai's, pulling him up. "Today was the day," he said simply.

Cai shook his head, still stunned by what had happened. Then he slapped dust off his tunic. "You were just lucky. Rufus said so," he growled. Then, his face cracked into a huge grin. "But you're getting to be a bonny fighter, Bear cub."

He glanced down at his slashed and stained fighting leathers. "Wait until my lord father sees me," he added ruefully, "and finds out who did it. He'll never let me live it down!"

"And your lady mother will never let me live it down that I've pinked her precious baby lamb!" returned Bear, grinning. They both roared with laughter. Cai threw his uninjured arm around Bear, and the two of them staggered off to look for Branwyn and her herbal plasters. The others drifted off in a group, leaving David alone. He gazed after them, half-wishing he could go along.

"Today was the day."

David turned. A wiry, dark-haired boy named Bedwyr had stayed behind with him. He jerked his thumb in the direction of the village, and together they turned that way. After a moment, David asked, "You mean Cai has always beaten Bear before?"

"Always," said Bedwyr. "Though anyone who watched Bear fight knew that wouldn't last forever."

"Why did Cai take it so well?" wondered David. "He's such a hot-head." And a bully, he added to himself.

"His temper matches his fiery thatch, doesn't it?" Bedwyr grinned. "But underneath all his bluster, he does love Bear, you know. After all, he's Bear's foster-brother. As am I."

"Where I come from that's not always a great thing to be."

"So? You come from a strange land, then. It's our custom that the sons of chieftains are raised in other chieftains' households. And they become like brothers to their sons. Often closer than birth brothers. Cai remains with his family because Lord Rhodri is powerful and will have it so. Bear and I have grown up with him since we were eight."

"Eight!"

"Of course. That's when we begin our training as warriors. I was sent here by my father then. As for Bear, well, Emrys just appeared with him one day soon after I arrived. For some reason, Lord Rhodri allowed him to stay, and right glad he is of it now, seeing how Bear has turned out."

David thought that over in silence. No wonder they were all so good at fighting. Bedwyr, though slender and not much taller than David, was a skilled warrior with sword and spear.

"If this isn't your home, where do you come from, Bedwyr?" he asked.

"Less Prydein, across the Narrow Sea." Bedwyr's face was suddenly grim. "My people still fight off the tribes that brought down the Romans. As soon as I can, I'll return to help them."

They took the path along the river. "There's a thing I'd like to know, Bedwyr," David ventured after a few minutes.

"Aye?"

"What Rufus said about Emrys. Some people are afraid of him, aren't they? Is he some kind of a wizard? And what did Rufus mean about being turned into a bat or an owl?"

Bedwyr stopped in his tracks and stared at David. "Why don't you ask Emrys yourself?" he said.

David shrugged. "I don't know. I don't dare to, I guess. I'd even feel funny asking Bear about it."

Bedwyr nodded. "Well, about Emrys. Many of these folk believe he's a mage, and maybe Emrys likes to let them think it. Bear says he's the wisest man in Prydein, but no wizard, and he should know. He's a great bard, certainly, and something of a healer. And he often goes on mysterious journeys, nobody knows where. More than that, I don't know. As to the owl, that's an old tale, and doesn't really have anything to do with Emrys."

He glanced sideways at David. "The owl follows you, doesn't it?" he said. "They say so in the village."

"Whenever I'm out at night. I try not to be. But I often hear an owl near the hut."

"Come, then," said Bedwyr, "and I'll tell you the story of the owl, for what it's worth."

They settled themselves on a mossy log on the riverbank.

"The story is about a wizard, named Gwydion," began Bedwyr. "Long ago, he agreed to help a youth who was under a doom never to marry a mortal woman. So Gwydion created a wife for the lad. Out of flowers."

"Flowers? Oh, come on!" David guffawed.

Bedwyr nodded. "It's true. Out of flowers of oak and broom and meadowsweet," he said. "They say she was the loveliest lady ever seen. Blodeuwedd, he named her. And she married the youth. But later she fell in love with another man and planned for her lover to murder her husband." He paused for a moment, then added, "It didn't work."

"So what happened?"

"The husband killed the man who had nearly killed him. And Gwydion turned Blodeuwedd into an owl to punish her. She flies between the worlds, they say. And goes a-hunting men's souls."

"And people think the owl that follows me is Blodeuwedd?" David shuddered. "Why would she hunt me? That old tale has nothing to do with me."

"That I don't know," said Bedwyr, getting up. He gave David a level look. "I know nothing about you. You're one who always keeps himself to himself, I think. But they say the Lady is drawn by black feelings, the kind she knew herself in life. Unhappiness, rage, confusion. And such folk she hunts to their doom."

I was feeling all of those things, David said to himself as they returned to the path. Have felt them for so long. And she came right into my world after me. And though she missed her hunting that night, she still . . . wants me. The thought made his blood run cold. Yet Emrys had said he might be wrong to fear the owl. It didn't make sense!

At the edge of the village, the child Arianrod raced out to meet them. "David's got a dirty face," she chanted shrilly. "Cai says he rubbed his nose in the dust!"

David scowled at her, but said nothing.

"Shut up, brat," said Bedwyr amiably. "David does well enough. And he's a guest and a bardling, too. So mind your tongue."

Arianrod picked up a pebble and bounced it off David's ankle. "Nyaaah," she said. "He's nought but an unchancy stranger living off our charity. My da says so!"

"Arianrod!" A tall girl poked her head out of a nearby hut. Her voice was clear and musical, but it cracked like a whip.

With a hasty look over her shoulder, Arianrod shied one more pebble at David and fled.

"That one's an imp of Annuvin, as you were at the same age," said Bedwyr with a grin as they came up to the girl. "David, this is Merioneth. Meri's been visiting her aunt, away up-river. This is David Baird, a stranger among us."

That face, thought David. Meri. MeriMeriMeri. He couldn't say a word.

Meri tossed her dark head. "Oh, but I already know him quite well. I helped Branwyn nurse him before I went away," she said lightly. "Do you remember?" she added, her eyes dancing as she gazed at David.

"Uh, sort of." Great! David thought. Now she'll think I'm stupid as well as strange. Then something occurred to him. He'd been wearing no clothes when he woke up. Surely she hadn't helped Branwyn undress and bathe him like a baby! The thought left him scarlet and even more tongue-tied.

As if she could read his mind, Meri grinned wickedly. "Yes, I should say I know you quite well," she said teasingly.

David bit his lip and looked down at the ground. He'd never met a girl as bold as this. She was awful.

"Meri, what devilry is this?" Bedwyr looked from one to the other of them. "Leave him alone. He's already had enough punishment for one day. As if Arianrod weren't enough, he's had a drubbing from Cai."

Meri nodded. "It's all over the village," she said, grinning. Then, seeing the look on David's face, she added, "Cai's not a bad person at heart. But he doesn't know when enough's enough. I'm sure he wouldn't mean to hurt you, knowing you're not used to our ways."

Oh, yeah? thought David. But he nodded and said, "Thanks."

Bedwyr raised a hand in farewell and left David to plod on alone. Arianrod had only put into words what he had already read in the faces of the villagers. They were suspicious of him. Feared him, even, because of the owl. And begrudged feeding a stranger. His heart sank. Where would he go if they turned him out? He'd never be able to survive alone in this wild country!

Emrys's hut stood empty. The bard was gone again, without notice,

With a sigh, David peeled off his soiled leathers and dashed water over himself from a basin. His arms and body were criss-crossed with fresh welts from Cai's cudgel, and the black-and-blue remains of earlier encounters.

Bruises on the bruises, he thought glumly. Then, as he reached for a clean tunic, he noticed a small bottle sitting beside the basin. He pulled out the stopper and sniffed. A pungent aroma tickled his nose. It was liniment, or something very like it. A scrap of parchment was under the bottle. On it was scrawled a message in rough letters. It read:

> I hear you need mending again. This is for bruises. rub it in well. It will hurt!
>
> B.

Branwyn, he thought, feeling a little less lonely. He poured liniment into his palm and began rubbing it in. The sting was fierce enough to make him gasp, yet somehow it comforted him.

EIGHT

W ho is that girl?"
"What girl?" asked Bear, only half listening. He was muttering under his breath as he scraped out the porridge pot that hung over the fire.

"Meri—whatsit."

Bear raised his eyebrows. "Merioneth. Just a girl. Gwyn, her father, is the clan smith. That makes him a big fellow around here. He's a hard man, and as hot-tempered as the fire in his forge. Why the sudden interest in Meri?"

"Nothing," said David quickly. "I just remember her nursing me back at the beginning. Bedwyr and I met her yesterday."

"Aye, she has a hand for the healing and helps Branwyn when her mam can spare her. Which isn't often."

David drank in every word, while trying not to look interested. Somehow, he couldn't get Meri out of his head.

"Here." Bear thrust a wooden bowl of porridge under his nose. "I wish Emrys would get back. I hate the taste of my own cooking."

"So do I," said David, feelingly. The porridge was half-burnt. "In my time we eat this stuff with gobs of cream and brown sugar and raisins on it. Though even that wouldn't help this garbage!"

Bear cuffed him lightly. "Ah, eat it, man, and stop whingeing! You'll be glad enough of it under your belt when you face Cai on the practice ground."

"That stinker! Don't remind me."

Bear grinned. "Nay, he's my foster-brother, as well you know. I'll not hear him ill-used. He's just a wee bit boisterous, is our Cai."

"He's a menace," grumbled David.

"You stand up well enough," said Bear. "You're no fighter, but you've got grit. Maybe that's what drives Cai to bait you. You're different, you see."

"I've figured that out, thanks," said David lightly. But his heart lifted at Bear's praise. Coming from him, it meant something. "I guess . . . I mean, I should thank you," he went on clumsily. "For making me practise all those weeks. Those guys would have done for me by now if you hadn't."

Bear shrugged. "The thought had crossed my mind," he admitted. "But I must say I felt like thrashing you myself sometimes, cocky devil that you are."

David grinned. "Don't worry. It felt like thrashing, even if you didn't mean it to be."

Bear threw his head back and laughed. "And mayhap did you a bit of good, did it?" he asked.

"I guess," said David.

Bear gestured with the hand that held the porridge bowl. "And what do you make of all this . . . now?" he asked, suddenly serious.

"It's still weird to me. The food. The clothes. And being an outsider." David picked up a stick to poke the fire. Then his eyes met Bear's gaze. "But then I suppose I was that before, too."

Bear held his glance for a minute, then nodded and returned to his porridge.

As soon as Bear left, David flung a cloak over his tunic and set off through the village. His feet seemed to take the direction of Meri's hut without his willing them to. He didn't find her, but saw a thin dark woman who must be her mother. Arianrod, who was grinding grain in a quern and managing to spill most of it, stuck her tongue out at him as he passed. David returned the compliment, then felt silly. What a pest that kid was!

The smithy stood not far away. David recognized the chinking sound he had heard so many times during his illness. The man wielding the hammer was tall and burly, with hair the colour of the bronze he was working. A knot of men stood gathered around him. They all looked up as David passed. He nodded, and a few of them nodded back grudgingly. The smith made some comment in a low voice and spat on the ground. The others laughed.

Embarrassed, David took the first turning he came to. It led toward the practice ground. He knew the others wouldn't be there yet, so he allowed his feet to carry him that way. Then he heard voices. Girls' voices. Maybe Meri . . . He stepped forward to the edge of the clearing.

And froze.

They were fighting. Pairs of girls in short tunics

circled each other, now and again slashing quickly with their daggers. Each had a thick cloth pad tied round her left forearm, and used it to parry the thrusts. Lithe and vicious as wildcats, they circled each other, pouncing with their daggers when an opening appeared. Some of them were little older than Arianrod. Some were much older, Meri among them.

A tall, burly woman with grizzled hair moved around them, encouraging and coaching. "Rhiannon, keep your guard up. That's better. Good, Olwen! Keep right after her. Elayne, you silly little cow, that dagger isn't a darning needle. Don't poke with it, stab with it!"

Two of the girls at the edge of the pack caught sight of David and stopped in their tracks. They glanced at each other and giggled. The giggles spread in ripples as other pairs stopped to see what was going on.

"Look, Gwyladys . . ." someone said, pointing.

The tall woman whirled about, scowling. Then her weathered face cracked into a huge grin. "Well, here's a handsome young rooster for the hen coop. Come to join us, have you, bardling? Mayhap that's not such a bad idea, seeing how badly Rufus's rabble treat you. Or so I hear."

The girls shrieked with laughter. David took one step backwards and plunged into the undergrowth.

Gwyladys's voice pursued him. "Nay, come back, my pretty. No need to be so shy."

These women, thought David, as he struggled through the bushes. These bloody awful women!

He blundered on until he reached the river. Throwing himself down on the bank, he splashed his burning face with water, groaning at the thought of the fool he'd made of himself. The news would be all over the village in half an hour.

Moments later, a twig snapped behind him, and he looked around. It was Meri. She said nothing, but with a sidelong glance sat down on the bank beside him and unwound the thongs that bound her leather sandals. She slid her feet into the water, then leaned forward and splashed her face. As she did so, he saw that her arms were criss-crossed by thin white lines. Old knife scars.

David shuddered. What kind of people were these, anyway?

She looked back at him out of those electric blue eyes. "You look . . . shocked," she said.

"I suppose I am."

She was puzzled. "Don't the women fight where you come from?"

"Not that way."

"How do they defend their homes in war, then?"

"They don't fight. Well, some are in the army . . . Oh, forget it. I can't explain," he snapped.

She said nothing more. After a minute or two, he glanced over at her. She gave an odd little hiccup, and for a moment he thought he'd upset her. Then he realized she was trying not to laugh.

Her control cracked. "You should have seen your face back there," she gasped, rolling on the bank. "Lord, it was funny. Better than the time Mam's pig got loose and ran under Lord Rhodri's horse, and him on it."

Stung, David jumped up. She got up too, frowning.

"Why are you looking like a thundercloud, then?

Don't tell me you're too high-and-mighty to take a jest!" she said indignantly.

David couldn't think of what to say, so he turned his back on her and stalked off with as much dignity as he could muster.

She bounded after him and gave him a great shove that caught him off balance. He stumbled, then whirled around.

She was standing with her back to the river, arms akimbo. "You're a poor sort of thing, aren't you?" she jeered. "Do something so daft it would make a cat laugh, then blame us for thinking it's funny. You make me mad, you do!" She shoved him again.

"You," spluttered David, "you're as bad as your brat of a sister!" He gave her a shove in return, and she lost her balance and tumbled backwards into the river.

She sat up waist-deep in the shallows and spat out a mouthful of water. After one stunned moment, David threw back his head and guffawed.

Meri sneezed. Then she smiled sweetly. "Give me a hand out of this, then," she said, wiping her nose.

Grinning, he leaned over reached out a hand.

She grabbed it and yanked him in.

They both went under. Then they sat up and looked at each other, water cascading down their faces.

"Are we quits, then?" asked Meri, pushing her sopping hair out of her eyes.

"Better be. I've swallowed half the river," grumbled David.

They helped each other up the bank. As they reached the top, Gwyladys popped out of the bushes. She looked them up and down and clicked her tongue. Then she sighed. "Aw, I might have known," she said. "The pretty boys aren't for me." She lumbered off down the path.

"Wow," breathed David, "she's really something. She could eat me for breakfast!"

Meri tossed her head. "Don't you forget for a moment she's only half joking," she said.

When David got back, Bear greeted him with a grin from ear to ear. "Well, I hear you got in a little extra training today. With the girls," he teased. Then, as David stood dripping by the fire, "By the by—aren't you a wee bit wet?"

"I fell in the river. Well, not exactly. I pushed Meri in. Then she pulled me in."

Bear opened his mouth, then closed it. "You pushed Meri in the river?" he asked in a choked voice.

David shrugged. "Well, sort of. She was being a real pain. Ragging me, you know. Then she gave me a shove. So I shoved her back, and she landed in the river."

Bear threw back his head and roared with laughter. When he could speak again, he gasped, "Well, you'll have every lad in the village on your side now. That minx has been making our lives miserable since we were all in nappies. But none of us could do a thing about it. Her father being the big man he is with Lord Rhodri. The river! Oh, that's grand, grand . . ." He went off into another peal of laughter.

Weird, thought David, rubbing himself dry with a prickly piece of sacking.

When he woke up the next morning, he blushed when he remembered what had happened. Then he lay there, grinning. She was something. She was gorgeous. She was outrageous. Then his smile faded. This thing was really getting hold of him. No one had ever made him feel this way, as if he didn't belong to himself anymore.

He tuned Beauty and set to work on the new ballad Emrys had taught him. It was a love song, and suddenly he found himself understanding the words in a new way. And that scared him.

When he saw Meri with the other girls later in the day, his heart gave a great leap. She greeted him gaily, and the others giggled. He passed the smithy again on his way to the practice ground. The smith glanced up and scowled at him. In tones loud enough for David to hear, he said to the men around him, "Young pup! I won't have him nosing after Meri, the dirty outlander."

Flushing, David went on towards the practice ground. Some of the young warriors chaffed him about joining the girls and getting the worst of it. They seemed friendly enough, though Cai and his friends still saw to it that David got a drubbing and ate dirt.

That night, with Emrys still away, Lord Rhodri summoned David. With his heart in his mouth, David tramped across to the hall. The spears clashed aside for him, and he approached the high table.

"My lady wife grows weary of battle chants," said the chieftain, leaning back in his chair and pulling his moustache. He nodded toward a slender brown-haired woman dressed in red who sat on his right hand.

Lady Eluned smiled down at David. "Can you oblige me with something sweeter to the ear, young man?" she asked pleasantly.

"Yes, my lady," said David. How can anyone that nice be that stinker Cai's mother? he wondered.

As he tuned Beauty, his eyes searched the hall for Meri. Then he found her. She was standing at the back with Bear and Cai and some of the others. Dressed in blue, her black braids bound with silver ribbons, she looked nothing like the tomboy of yesterday. But when she caught him staring, she gave him a bold wink.

He sang, and the thought of her twined itself into his music. First he gave them something funny. Then a thrilling tale of love. And when it was done, Lady Eluned clapped and Lord Rhodri nodded, well-pleased. Behind them, Cai slouched, scowling. Meri simply stood and stared at him wide-eyed, as though she had never seen him before.

David returned her gaze for a long moment, then, after bowing to Lord Rhodri and his lady, he plunged out of the hall into the welcome darkness. His heart was beating wildly. I can't feel like this about her! he told himself furiously. I can't. I mustn't!

NINE

I've got to go back." David stared across the fire at the others. Bear was mending a piece of battle harness. Emrys, with Beauty cradled on his lap, was staring into the flames.

"Back? But you can't . . ." Bear frowned. "Oh. You mean back to where I found you?"

David nodded. "There's a chance, just a chance that if I go back there something might happen. Nothing's going to happen here. Or it would have happened already."

Emrys shook his head. "I don't think it will work, lad."

"But it might," David said desperately. "What else can I do? You say you can't help me. And I can't just go on like this. I've got to know one way or the other. I've got to. I can't explain, exactly. But I've got to know. Now."

Emrys studied him for a long moment, then nodded.

"Why this sudden rush to be quit of us?" asked Bear. "I thought you were getting used to us—barbarians," he added slyly.

David met his gaze briefly before lowering his eyes. "Maybe it's because I am that I—oh, I don't know!" he said miserably.

Bear sighed. "So, another stroll in the woods for me, I suppose. You're not thinking you could make the trip alone?"

David grinned. "I may be dumb, but I'm not *that* dumb."

Emrys returned Beauty to its shelf. "Take bread and dried meat from my stores," he offered. "Enough for a few days. It should take you no longer than that."

"We won't need much," agreed Bear. "I can always catch a coney or two. And if I can't, Cabal can."

They left the next morning. As they tramped through the village they saw Meri in the distance. She waved. David raised his hand, but kept on walking. This was no time to think of Meri. If he did, he'd never have the courage to leave!

At the edge of the forest, he glanced back at the village, remembering how he had seen it the first time. It seemed different to him now—almost welcoming. He had found so much there. Meri. Beauty. Would he ever see either of them again?

"Are you coming or not?" asked Bear, shifting his pack impatiently.

"Coming," said David.

Bear. That's another thing, he thought, as he followed him into the forest. Bear mattered too. If this hunch worked and he went back to his own time, he'd never see Bear again. It would be back to all that . . . mess. David shivered. Did he really want to go back?

But how could he not try?

They camped the first night in a glade deep in the forest. Bear set snares and caught two rabbits for their supper. "Thanks, little brothers," he said, stroking their fur. "Your lives for our need." After a moment, he took out his knife and set about cleaning them.

"I remember your talking to a tree that other time," said David, who was picking up stones to ring the fire. "I thought you were nuts."

Bear looked up, grinning. "And now?"

"Sure of it. Ouch!" Bear had bounced a piece of bark off his ear.

"Emrys says it's well to remember we're only part of things," Bear said, returning to his cooking. "Not lords and masters over everything in nature. People used to know that long ago, but now we seem to be forgetting."

"It's even worse in my time."

Dusk fell. The late spring night was damp, and David wrapped his cloak more closely around him. The wood was alive with odd noises and rustlings. A fox barked not far away, and in the distance an owl hooted.

David met Bear's eyes across the fire. "Do you think . . . ?" he began.

Bear shrugged. "If it were the Lady, she'd come closer than that. Anyway, why worry? What more can she do to you than she's done already?"

"I'm not sure I want to find out," replied David, with a shiver.

They rolled themselves in their cloaks and lay down by the dying fire, Bear's head pillowed on Cabal's shaggy flank.

I'm crazy, David told himself. I should be hoping for the Lady to come. After all, she got me here. How can I get back without her? He lay awake for a long time thinking about it, before drifting off to sleep.

The next day, they reached the glade where David had first met Bear.

"Might as well camp where I did before," said Bear, slinging down his pack. "If you're determined to go through with this, we should do everything the same."

They lit a fire, but somehow neither of them felt much like eating. They fed the last of the cold rabbit to Cabal, then sat in silence as the light drained out of the world and the darkness rose up from the ground.

At last, Bear got up. "It's getting late," he warned. "If you want to be where you were when it happened, I'd best take you."

David nodded.

It took Bear only a few minutes to find the spot where the old track crossed the woods. "This was the place we came to in the morning," he said, standing on the path and sighting toward the great tree that loomed ahead of them in the dusk.

David took a few steps off the track and looked up into the branches of the tree where the owl had perched. "I must have been about here when I woke up."

"Then I'll leave you," said Bear. "I must, if this scheme is to work." He put both hands on David's shoulders. "If it does . . ." His voice trailed off. Then, "Good luck," he said, gruffly. Whistling to Cabal, he disappeared into the undergrowth.

David almost called him back. He shivered, and tugged his cloak more closely about him. He couldn't see anything, not even the faintest glow from Bear's fire. It must be late. How late had it been that night? Eleven? Twelve?

He didn't notice the wood go still around him, or hear the rustle of wings. But something told him he was being watched. He turned, and there it was. Cloud-white, the owl sat preening itself on a low-hanging branch.

"You did follow us," David breathed. "Lady, I'm sorry for what I did before. Send me back. I don't belong here. Please!"

The owl cocked its head, for all the world as though it were listening. It ruffled its feathers and settled them. Then it spread its wings and floated silently away, a white spot growing fainter in the darkness, then gone.

David stared into the gloom, hoping to see the trees melt away and ghost lights spring up along the haunted path. Nothing. At last he threw himself down on the ground, burying his head in his arms. After a long time, he slept.

He awoke when a foot slid under his ribs and flipped him onto his back. Bear grinned down at him. In the east, the rising sun sent shafts of green-gold light through the trees.

"Didn't work, did it?" crowed Bear. "I needn't have worried. Emrys said it would be so."

Cabal pushed past his master's knees and greeted David with a large, sloppy lick.

"Oof-ugh! Get away, you great horse," spluttered David, wiping his face on his arm.

Bear stretched a hand to pull him to his feet.

"You . . . worried?" David asked.

The brown-gold eyes held his, quizzically. Then Bear shrugged. "Aye," he said.

"She did come, you know. The Lady. But she wouldn't take me," said David.

Bear's eyes widened, then he nodded. "Perhaps . . . perhaps she isn't finished with you yet," he said.

There was a moment of silence. Then, David said, "Well, I'm kind of glad to see your homely mug again, too."

Bear clapped him so hard on the shoulder that he reeled. "No need to blather on about it, man," he said. "Here's breakfast." He handed him a hunk of bread. "Then let's climb above the woods for a look-about before we go back"

They came up out of the trees, Cabal bounding ahead of them, and climbed silently toward the great stone ruin that loomed above them on the bare ridge. They pushed their way through waist-high bracken and golden gorse. Away from the shelter of the trees, the sun was hot, and the air was thick with the scent of heather in bloom. Sweat ran down David's brow and trickled under the scratchy cloth of his tunic.

Yet in the shadow of the stones it was chilly. David stared at the gaunt shapes rearing against the sky. This was what he had seen in the distance on that moon-bright night. This was the spot toward which the lights had climbed out of the dark valley. Just before his world went crazy.

Bear placed his hands flat on the lichen-covered stone. Closing his eyes, he rested his forehead against it. David watched him for a moment, then did the same, straining to hear an echo of far-off singing. He heard only the whine of wind among the stones and the humming of the bees in the heather. A feeling of emptiness overwhelmed him.

Bear cast himself down on the springy turf where Cabal lay panting, pillowed his head on the hound's back, and, closing his eyes, turned his face up to the sun. "Are you very disappointed?" he asked.

"Yes. No. I don't know." David squatted beside him and gazed out over the sweep of the wooded valley below. "I mean, I know I don't belong here." He paused.

"But . . ?"

"I don't know how to say it, exactly. It sounds crazy, but being here is like being given a fresh start. With no mistakes counted against me."

Bear's mouth quirked at one corner.

"Well," David added quickly, "not so many, anyway."

"Your past does seem to be behind you," Bear agreed. "Or rather, ahead of you."

"It's more than that, though," David went on. "I've lived in cities all my life and never given a hoot about nature. But here the woods, the hills, the river—they feed something in me. Something I didn't know was hungry. Something to do with my music."

"Spoken like a bard," said Bear, sitting up and stretching. "It sounds like poetry to me."

"It's just . . . your world's so green, Bear. So . . . so unspoiled." David gestured toward the valley below. "Like here. It's so different now from the way it was. I mean, the way it will be," he said. "In my time all the trees are gone. Only this hasn't changed." He jerked his thumb at the stones behind them.

"It's already as old as time," said Bear. "I'm glad

there's something I know that doesn't change. But I can't imagine living in a world that wasn't green. Still, your world has all the other things you've told me about . . ." His voice trailed away. He shaded his eyes to gaze at the pale wafer of moon floating in the western sky. "Like the men who will walk . . . there."

David grinned. "That's your favourite of all my tales, isn't it? That and the dinosaurs."

"I like best things that seem impossible. Emrys says it will be my greatest failing in life." Bear grinned back. "And my greatest gift. Though I believe you when you tell me these impossible things are true," he added. "I know you wouldn't lie. And you never tell these tales to anyone but me."

"Emrys said not to."

"He's right," said Bear soberly. "Our folk love wonder tales. But if the tales are frightening, then the teller might be blamed. Best to stick to your singing."

"But you're not frightened. And you believe me."

"Frightened? Sometimes, when you talk, I'm drunk with the excitement of it!" Bear threw his arms out, gesturing widely. "It's like, it's like . . . owning the world," he went on. "You've told me things that even Emrys doesn't know. I feel as if I can see forever. The future. The past. Not just dinosaurs and moon men, but pyramids and skyscrapers, and knights and castles."

"And computers and television and jumbo jets."

"Yes. Yes." Bear hugged his knees tightly and watched the cloud shadows chase each other across the hills.

"But why do you care so much about it all, Bear?" David asked. "I mean, most people in the village wouldn't. Oh, they'd ask a few questions. But then they'd forget. Or they'd expect me to tell them how many pigs there'd be in the next litter!"

Bear glanced at David almost shyly. "I've this feeling that it's for something," he replied.

David was puzzled. "What do you mean?"

"I've never told this to anybody, mind. Not even Emrys, though I daresay he knows all the same. I may be daft, but I've always felt there's something I'm supposed to do. Or try to do. Except I don't know what it is yet. And this is for that, somehow . . ." His voice trailed off. Then, "Over there! See it?" he said suddenly, pointing.

David shaded his eyes against the glare. At first he could make out nothing. Then, high above the valley, he saw a bird riding the wind. "Is it Blodeuwedd come back?" he asked.

"Of course not, numbskull. Owls hunt by night. It's an eagle, by its size," said Bear. "That's it exactly," he added, half to himself.

"What?"

Bear turned to look at David, his eyes wide. "How I feel. The eagle's like you, David. He sees across the high hills the way you see across time. Through you, I see the landscape of time. Once and future time . . ."

David watched the bird until it dropped out of sight beyond a distant ridge. "I can't see what use it is to you to know all that stuff," he said at last. "Or what good it is for me to remember it, now I'm stuck here for the rest of my life." Then he added ruefully, "Maybe it would be better if I forgot!"

"I'm glad you can't," said Bear. He stood up, and

looked down at David searchingly. "You've given me something I've never had before. Something that helps me make sense of things. Now I know that there's more than our enemies, our fears, our little quarrels among ourselves. That things don't have to stay the same. That terrible wars are fought, but marvellous things happen too. Knowing that . . . helps."

"I can't think why," said David, getting up.

Bear put a hand on his shoulder. "Never mind, bardling," he said. "Let's go home."

TEN

David's fingers stumbled over the harp strings. He took a deep breath and tried the run again. Failed again.

Blast! he thought. What's the matter with me? I've done this before! Annoyed, he set Beauty down a little too hard, and the harp's strings twanged in protest.

Emrys winced. "Stop torturing my harp! If you're more ham-handed than usual today, you've no-one to blame but yourself."

David jumped up. Biting back angry words, he paced back and forth, rubbing the back of his neck. "Sorry," he mumbled at last. "I don't know what's got into me."

"No?" said Emrys dryly, looking up at him. "I'd have said you aren't paying attention to what you're doing."

"I am, too," David began hotly. Then stopped. He wasn't. His thoughts had wandered off again. To Meri.

"A bard needs more than moonshine between his ears," said Emrys severely. "You're getting nowhere. Wasting my time. And I won't have it." He got up, drawing his cloak around him and stood looking down at David from under his shaggy brows. "I can't have it," he added in a lower voice. "There is great need to bind the tribes, lest the Saxons destroy us separately. That is my work, and I am sorely pressed. You can help, if you will, but not if you don't give your heart to the work."

David hung his head.

Emrys sighed. "Well. Before I teach you any more, you'll learn a thousand lines of that genealogy I gave you. As proof that you're willing to work at minstrelsy."

"A thousand lines! But that's . . ."

"Silence!" roared Emrys. "A thousand, I say. Perhaps that will focus your wits. And until you've done as I say, leave Beauty alone." Seizing his staff, he strode out, muttering under his breath.

David mumbled a few choice words of his own. A thousand lines—that would take him weeks! He kicked Emrys's chair halfway across the hut. After a moment, though, he picked it up and set it back in its place.

Emrys is right, he thought. I'm not getting anywhere. But how can I, when she, when she . . .

Meri was driving him crazy. Oh, she'd seemed pleased enough to see him when he and Bear got back. Her face had lit up as she gazed at him.

"I thought you'd gone," she said.

"I tried losing him in the woods, but he followed me home," said Bear, grinning.

She made a face at him. "You'll be staying, then?" she asked David.

"If they'll let me."

"I'm glad," she said, as she turned away.

But the next time they met, she was with some other girls, and she greeted him with no more than a nod and a toss of the head. Then she whispered something to the girl next to her, who giggled. David flushed and walked away.

Another day, when he was rinsing the porridge pot at the river, Meri and her friends peered down at him from the bank.

"Fine mess you're making of that," Meri said critically. "Don't you know to soak it, then rub it with clean sand?"

"Uh, no."

"Men!" she said scornfully. "And I can see your clothes need washing too. I can imagine what kind of a sty your hut is, with the three of you great louts penned up together!"

The others shrieked with laughter as they set about scrubbing up their own pots.

She thinks I'm a fool after all, David thought, confused. But the next time he passed her hut, she stopped him and asked, almost shyly, about his music. And then gave him such a glance through her long lashes that he felt as if he'd been struck by blue lightning.

After that he'd often made lame excuses to walk that way, his heart sinking when he didn't see her. He had to be near her, to touch her. Had to. But there seemed to be no way. All he could do was dream over the harp, singing every love ballad he knew. Seeing her face as he sang. Hoping she would come to him. But she never did.

He asked himself why a thousand times. It wasn't as if village girls stayed locked away. Why, everywhere he looked, women were striding about on their business, laughing, talking, quarrelling with each other and the men. They looked you straight in the eye and said exactly what they thought. So did Meri, when others were around. But she never sought him out alone.

Sometimes he almost convinced himself that he'd only imagined she cared for him. Then they'd meet somehow by chance, and she'd give him that shining look.

Now, angry at Emrys and even more at himself, he flung out of the hut. After a few steps, he stopped, cursing, then went back for a copy of the lines he had to memorize. Might as well get on with it, he told himself grimly.

He set off along the path that followed the river. But he kept meeting people—a woman who nodded to him in a friendly way, a man who scowled, then some girls who giggled at his greeting. He turned off into the woods, taking first one path, then another, scarcely aware of the direction he was taking. He strode along, matching his stride to the rhythm of the lines he was trying to pound into his head.

It wasn't until he'd mastered a chunk of the text that he stopped and looked around. He was in a glade he couldn't remember. Idiot, he told himself, trying to remember which path he had taken. If you've gone and lost yourself, you'll never hear the end of it.

Then he heard it. Singing. Clear and joyous as a lark, liquid as water rilling over stones. And he knew without question whose voice it was, though he'd never heard it sing before. He dashed across the clearing, tearing his way through the bracken. Which direction was it coming from?

The voice stopped.

"Meri!" he cried, looking around desperately. "Meri, where are you? It's me, David! Can you hear me?"

He'd almost given up looking when she stepped from the shadow of a tree right at his elbow. "Hear you?" she asked, tossing her head. "Folk could hear you in Isca, the noise you're making!"

"Meri!" he said, grinning foolishly, delightedly. "This is great! I was just thinking about you." Then he added, half-embarrassed, "I was trying to memorize some lines Emrys set me. But you kept getting tangled up in them somehow."

"So? And why would that be?" Her eyes widened innocently. Too innocently.

"Oh . . . you! You know how I feel about you. You must. It's written all over me. I love you. And you . . . you love me too. I know it!" Then, as the laughter left her eyes, he stammered, "I . . . I mean, I do know it, don't I?"

"Love you? Do I, then?" She looked at him levelly. It was a real question. Then she stepped forward to kiss him. Not a shy, girlish brush of the lips, but a long, slow considering kiss.

He was so startled, he almost forgot to kiss back.

At last, she pulled away. "Yes," she said softly, answering her own question. "Yes, I think I do."

"Oh, Meri!" David put his arms about her, pinning her against the trunk of the tree. And this time he made the most of his opportunity.

She pushed him away, at last, and they stood looking at each other, breathless. Then they turned back to the glade and sat down on a mossy log. He put his arm about her, thrilled to have her to himself at last, beside him. He didn't even want any more . . . yet. Now that he knew there would be time for it all. Now that he knew she loved him.

"Sing to me, David," she said softly. "Just for me. I love to hear your voice. It was when you sang that I first thought I loved you."

"You sing with me," he replied.

He began, one of the love songs he had dreamed over for so many days. Meri picked up the harmony, her voice twining with his like ivy round holly. David thought his heart would burst with happiness. They sang and stopped to kiss, and kiss again, and touch. Then they sang on, the late afternoon sun gilding them with light. They never noticed a figure who, drawn to the edge of the glade by their voices, stood frozen, listening awhile, before disappearing back into the shadow of the trees.

At last, as the sun touched the treetops, Meri sighed. "We must go back," she said, looking about. "Now where's my basket? I dropped it when I heard your crashing and shouting. At first I thought it was a Saxon coming after me! Branwyn will scold if I don't bring her the herbs she asked for."

He helped her find the basket, then they set off. It was strange how clearly marked the path seemed now that they were together. He walked behind her through the trees, drinking in the grace of her, her lightness of foot. All too soon he could hear the sounds of the village ahead.

Hungry for one last touch of her, he reached out and pulled her into his arms again. "Meri, I'm so glad! Everything's going to be so different now. Why didn't you let me know you cared for me so much? When you knew perfectly well how much I loved you." He gave her a little shake.

To his surprise, she drew away. In the twilight, her eyes looked enormous. "Why?" she asked. "Because I'd hoped to avoid what happened today. I'd hoped to spare you, *cariad*. And myself, too."

"Avoid! Meri, this is the happiest day of my life!"

She reached out and pressed her hand against his cheek, in a gesture so tender it made him shiver. He turned the palm of her hand and kissed it.

After a moment, she drew it away. "I'm glad I've given you that, at least," she said. "Because it's all I can give you. Ever."

"All? But you love me! You said you did!"

She nodded, her eyes cast down. "I do. And it's wicked bad of me. No one must ever know. For your sake as much as mine."

"Wrong? But why?"

"Because I am to be wed to someone else. At the next Beltane festival."

"No!" he said. "I . . . I don't believe you."

"Dear David, I'm so sorry." She reached out as if to touch him again, then stopped. "Oh, I've tried not to show how I feel. Hoped you'd find out I wasn't free, and understand. That Bear, Bedwyr—someone—would tell you! It's been arranged between our families for ever so long, since we were babies, almost."

"You mean you're still going to marry someone else now? When you know you love me? That's crazy!"

"You don't understand our ways. I must. It's a question

of honour. Mine. His. Both our families'."

"Just tell me who it is. I'll talk to him. Fight him if I have to. I'll make him give you up!"

"It can't be." She turned away.

"Meri!" he shouted after her. "Who is it?"

She stopped short. "It's Cai," she said in a choked voice. Without looking back, she walked on into the village.

ELEVEN

They're coming! The war band from upriver!" A pack of children, Arianrod at their head, raced shrieking down the main street of the village. Dogs barked, and chickens and pigs clucked and squealed as they were shooed hastily out of the way.

Brooding alone in Emrys's hut, David ignored the uproar until Bear poked his head in and said, "Come on, Longface. This is a sight you shouldn't miss."

David shrugged and set Beauty down. With Emrys still away, there was no one to say no. As he stepped outside, Bear added, "It's not every year the High King summons a war hosting. That's something to thank the Saxons for, I suppose!"

The square of pounded earth outside Lord Rhodri's hall was packed with men and horses, and wagons were still rolling in. The warriors from upriver were mingling with Rhodri's band, greeting and chaffing each other. The sun blazed off polished helms and spear points. Glints of light danced on the silver and gilt embroidery of bridles and pennons, and the crimson, gold, and blue of the warriors' tall shields glowed.

Rhodri, ready to mount, was bidding goodbye to

Lady Eluned. Cai stood beside his mother, a black scowl on his face. David's eyes flew at once to Meri, standing just behind them. Then he looked away.

Bedwyr grinned as Bear and David came up. "Look at Cai," he said, jerking a thumb at him. "Couldn't believe his father would leave him at home this time. He'll have be content with training battles for another year."

"Like the rest of us," said Bear. His brown eyes looked wistful.

"You're crazy, all of you!" said David sharply. "Why be in such a hurry to get yourselves killed? It's war they're going to, not a party!"

"What, bardling, after all the stirring battle songs you and Emrys have been singing us?" teased Bear. "We'd have to be made of stone not to yearn to test our swords against the foe!"

"That's different. That's . . . poetry," said David. Noble deeds did seem different when they were set to stirring music. But to actually ride out looking for wounds and maybe death? No thanks. This bloodthirstiness was something he'd never understand about these people.

"It's not so much that we enjoy killing," said Bear, as if reading his mind. "Though we enjoy a good fight. Or a good cattle-raid. But now it's a question of protecting British people in the Land of Summer from cold-blooded murder. That's what the High King is trying to do. That's why he's calling up all his warriors."

"Murder? Really?" David raised his eyebrows disbelievingly.

"Yes. You can't imagine how bad the fighting is in the east and south." Bear met his eyes gravely. "Don't forget,

I've seen it." He turned away and said nothing more. David and Bedwyr exchanged glances. Bear rarely referred to his past before Emrys brought him to the village.

Rhodri swung into the saddle. Raising a gauntleted hand, he signalled the riders to move off. As he passed the group around Bear, he called, "Your turn next year, lads. I promise. Meanwhile you and Cai are trusted to keep the village safe."

Bear nodded, raising his hand in farewell.

They watched until the last wagon had jolted off in its cloud of dust. Then a voice said behind them, "We'll do more than that. Who's for hunting the black boar?"

It was Cai, with his hangers-on behind him. Cheers and shouts greeted his words.

"You heard your father," Bear said. "This is no time to go hunting."

"And wait weeks until the war band returns? And then have them hunt the boar and get all the glory for that too?" Cai spat in the dirt. "Well, foster-brother, if you're not brave enough, stay behind. You can take care of the children and old folks. Not that they need it. With British war hosts on the move everywhere there won't be an enemy within a hundred miles of here."

A murmur of agreement greeted his words. Bear glanced at Bedwyr, who shrugged.

Seeing him hesitate, Cai tried a different tack. "Ah, come on, Bear. You know that boar has been doing damage on the high farms. My father himself said it had to be hunted down. So come. It won't be the same without you and Bedwyr," he wheedled. "If we leave early tomorrow, we needn't even be gone overnight. What d'you say?"

"Well . . ." Bear looked at Bedwyr again. Suddenly, they both grinned, and Bear turned quickly back to Cai. "If it's less than a day. And if you swear we'll turn back if the beast runs too far from the village . . ."

"Good man!" Cai clapped him on the shoulder. He spun around and raised his arms. "Sharpen your spears, lads," he shouted, to the others. "It'll be roast boar for dinner tomorrow and a fine tale to tell the war band when they return."

Whooping gleefully, the young warriors made for their huts.

Cai turned back, his eyes narrowed. "And what about you, milksop?" he said viciously to David. "Are you going to come along and prove yourself a man? Or are you going to stay home with the womenfolk?"

"Oh, leave David alone," snapped Bedwyr. "What's it to you whether he goes or stays? Let him do as he pleases."

Cai hooked his thumbs in his sword belt and grinned. "Just wanted to see what he's made of, now that Rufus and Emrys aren't around to protect him," he sneered. "I've always thought he was lily-livered. Now we'll all know."

"Stop it!" Meri bounded forward to tug on Cai's arm. "Don't do this," she said, gazing up at him. "It's hateful. There's no need, Cai!"

No need! Sudden unreasoning rage boiled up inside David. Cai with his swaggering and boasting was what Meri thought was man enough to marry. It made him sick to think of them together. "I'll go," he said in a choked voice.

"Oh-ho!" crowed Cai, shaking off Meri's hand. "Our little singing cockerel has some fight in him, after all! Won't he just frighten that nasty big, bad boar!" He swaggered off, laughing.

Meri turned to David. "Don't be a fool," she said. "Don't let him goad you into it." She stared at him beseechingly for a moment, then walked swiftly away.

"She's right," said Bear. "Boar hunts are always dangerous. The beasts are so unpredictable. And you're no expert with a spear. No one will think the worse of you if you don't go."

"I said I'd go, and I'm going," said David tightly. "I know you all think I'm a coward. I'll show you!"

Bedwyr put his hand on David's shoulder. "Nay, David. None of us who knows you thinks that. We know your ways are not ours."

Angrily, David shook off his hand. Bedwyr gave a low whistle of surprise. "Touchy, aren't you?" he asked. "What's the matter? You've been acting like a gored ox for days."

David shrugged. As he turned away, Bear's words followed him.

"I'm beginning to have a shrewd suspicion about what's wrong," he said to Bedwyr. "Anyway, let's just do our best to make sure nothing happens to him tomorrow."

David cursed under his breath. Now they thought they had to baby-sit him!

In the grey light of early morning, he woke to the

echoing of horns and the deep baying of boarhounds. Grimly, he stuck a long dagger in his belt and picked up two casting spears. He found Bear and Bedwyr with the rest of the young warriors at the edge of the village. Their glances of concern as they greeted him made his stomach feel even more queasy with fear than it had been already. He nodded to them, saying nothing.

"The boar was last seen up near Owain's field," Cai bellowed above the hubbub. "We should be able to pick up the trail there."

They set off, the hounds straining at their leashes. They followed the river path for a while, then cut through the woods to come up on higher ground, where Lord Rhodri's folk cultivated a few fields. There they spread out in groups, each one casting about along the forest edge, hoping to pick up the boar's trail.

After a quarter of an hour, voices shouted and a pack of hounds began to yelp.

"They've found it!" Bear's voice was tense with excitement. "Come on! Hurry!"

Cai was already examining the trail. "The dung is fresh," he said, grinning up at them. "No older than last night. I'll wager he's lying up in a thicket somewhere," he added, gesturing toward the densest part of the forest. "Let the hounds loose."

Slipping their leads, the hounds raced, baying, under the dark eaves of the forest. Scrambling, cursing, stumbling, the hunters struggled through the bracken to keep up with them.

The sun stood high in the sky by now, and though the forest leaves shaded them, the air was clinging and damp under the trees. After a brave start, the hounds lost the scent and cast about from side to side trying to pick it up again.

"It's the accursed heat and damp," said Bear. "The beast must have been using this part of the wood for weeks. Now even the old trails are giving off scent. It's enough to put the dogs off."

Fine by me, thought David, panting and wiping his forehead on his sleeve.

The hours wore on as they quartered the thickest patch of woodland, stopping only to swallow a mouthful of bread and a swig of water from the flasks they carried. Then the hounds gave tongue and they were off again. David found himself left behind in a small glade with the main body of the hunt well ahead of him.

Who cares? he thought angrily, looking about. Let them go chasing all over this blasted wood. I'm better alone.

But he was not alone.

Even before he whirled about, he knew it surely. At first, he only sensed the danger. Then a monstrous black shape broke from cover to rush straight for him. He froze, unable to cast his spear or to leap aside. For a moment he felt outside himself, as if he were watching a freeze-frame from a movie. The boar. Himself. The inevitable line of collision. This is what death looks like, he thought.

Then a spear whizzed past from behind him, so close that he could feel the breath of its passing on his cheek.

The boar squealed hideously and veered off toward the undergrowth, a spear trailing from its shoulder. So quickly had it all happened that David still stood rooted to the spot. Then, hearing Bear's voice cursing richly and explicitly behind him, he began to shake.

"Wounded! That makes him more dangerous than ever," said Bear. And then he swore again. "I couldn't get a killing throw at him for fear of hitting you, you great daft booby," he scolded David. "What were trying to do, stare him down?" He picked up his spear, which lay where the boar had plunged into the bracken and inspected the bloodied blade. Then he added, "Well there'll be no difficulty tracking him now, for certes. He'll leave a well-marked trail enough!"

"Bad work, Bear. The beast should be dead," said Cai, who had raced up with Bedwyr and the others. "Oh, I know it's not your fault. It's his," he added, turning a hostile stare on David. "I'd be willing to bet he was too scared to move. Had to be rescued. Yes?"

Then, as David and Bear stood silent, he shouted to the others, "Get the hounds on the trail. We'll get him now. But be careful—he's wounded and twice-dangerous!"

Sick at heart, David followed the others. The bloody trail led through the wood to a heavily-thicketed dell. Baying wildly, the hounds surrounded it, making short dashes into the brush before backing out again.

"Let me finish him, if I can," said Bear grimly. "It was I who wounded him, so the risk must be mine."

Cai opened his mouth as if to protest, then closed it with a snap. "Right. Fan out, everyone. Stay alert. We don't know where he'll break cover. He'll be maddened with pain, and reckless with it."

They encircled the thicket, Bear taking up his position where the trail of blood disappeared into the bushes.

"Hai, hai!" The warriors began to whoop and chant, clashing their heavy spears against their shields as they moved slowly toward the thicket. Somebody hurled a rock into the bushes. The baying of the hounds was background to the awful din.

For a few moments, nothing happened. Then the boar charged out, his black bulk spewing blood. He hurled himself straight at Bear, flakes of foam spraying from his jaws. Bear stood where he was. No one sprang to help him. Horrified, David raised his spear and started forward.

Bear must have seen him out of the corner of his eye, for he shouted, "Stay back, you fool!"

The boar saw David too, and veered for a moment in its charge. Bear flung himself sideways to compensate. The point of his spear, plunging into the boar's throat, seemed to sink in forever, driven by the force of the beast's charge. Bear went down on one knee, bracing himself. The impaled boar screamed in agony and thrashed wildly, trying to reach its tormentor.

Bear, thrown off balance, fell, just as the boar's tusks slashed sideways. The other hunters rushed forward, hurling their spears into the animal's body. It gave a convulsive shudder and died. A great shout of triumph went up, making the rooks caw and flap away through the trees.

David stood over Bear. He lay white-faced, clutching his left leg, which was deeply gashed.

"Bear! I'm sorry, I'm sorry!" gasped David, dropping to his knees beside him. "I thought you'd be killed! I wanted to help you, but I only made it worse. I've let you down again."

Bear spoke through gritted teeth. "Never . . . mind."

Nothing has changed, David told himself bitterly. I always fail everyone. Always.

Cai shoved David aside and, slashing a strip of cloth off his tunic, began to bandage Bear's leg. His big hands were oddly gentle. But there was nothing gentle about the look he gave David. "I should have known. You had to come, didn't you? Because I dared you," he said scornfully. "But not to take care of yourself, to bear a man's part, oh no. Just to show off. You leave it to others to save your precious skin. So Bear wounded the boar saving you, and in honour he had to risk his life to bring it down. Then you blundered in and turned the boar's charge. I hope you're satisfied."

David stared bleakly at the boar. Its bloodshot eyes, wide open, glared up at him. Even in death it was terrifying, yet somehow pitiful. It stank of blood and dung. Cai pulled out his knife and slit the boar's belly from throat to tail. The steaming entrails slid onto the ground.

David's stomach heaved, and he threw up on the grass. Cai gave him a glance of disgust, then turned back to his butchering.

By the time the gutted boar was hoisted on spears for the return trip to the village, it was late afternoon. The clammy heat had increased, and the hunters cursed and grumbled as they tramped through the undergrowth, brushing away stinging insects attracted by the blood of their kill.

"See how dark it's getting," said Bedwyr, glancing upward. He and David were taking turns to support the limping Bear.

"It's too early for sunset," said Bear. "It's a storm, surely."

"Look at the dogs," ventured David. "What's wrong with them? They're acting as if they're afraid of something."

It was true. The great hounds, usually so savage, were slinking along, ears lowered, tails between their legs. They pressed as close as possible to the legs of the hunters, who cursed and whipped them off with thongs.

"Just sated on the boar's offal, maybe," said Bedwyr. "Still, it seems odd . . ."

A savage gust of wind roared over the forest, making the trees creak and sway. "Just our luck," groaned Bear. "It's a storm, all right, and we're still a mile or two above the village."

"At least we're clear of the trees," said Bedwyr, as they came out on the river path. "But we're in for a drenching."

A bolt of lightning sizzled across the sky and thunder rolled along the valley. Dark clouds boiled down toward them from the heights.

"Listen!" cried Bear suddenly. "Do you hear it?"

For a moment, David thought he meant the thunder. Then he heard it too. Down from the top of the sky echoed the winding of a horn. It seemed to come from an unimaginable distance. And as if in response came another sound—the hideous yelping of a huge pack of hounds.

"The dogs! They've gone crazy!" cried David, whirling around. But their own hounds lay cowering on the ground. The other hunters stared into the boiling sky, their faces white and strained as the awful yelping drew nearer.

Bear shouted. "It's the Hounds! Down! Everybody down! Whatever you do, don't look!" He threw himself flat on the muddy path, dragging David with him.

David raised his head to peer up into the gloom. At first, there was only the hideous sound. Then he saw them. Hounds. Huge hounds, pale against the clouds, with fiery red eyes and red-lined ears and mouths. Jaws agape and slavering foam, they raced high overhead on the wings of the storm, driven down the valley by the terrible sound of that unseen horn.

David felt the hair on the nape of his neck bristle with fear. Then Bear pushed his head down. "Didn't you hear me? It's inviting death to look on them!" he snarled.

David buried his face in his arms as the ghostly hunt raced over. Gradually the baying died away down the valley. Thunder rolled again, and a cold rain sheeted down.

Silently, the hunters clambered to their feet. They stood staring at one another out of stricken mud-smeared faces. Even Cai looked ashen.

David shook Bear by the shoulder. "What were those things? What were they hunting?" he shouted over the rain, his voice cracking.

Bear stared back at him. "They're the Hounds of

Annuvin, the hunting pack of the Lord of the Underworld. They hunt the spirits of the newly dead," he said slowly. "But I don't . . ."

He faced down river, into the wet wind. Then, "Sweet Lord of Light," he cried, "don't you smell it? Smoke!"

TWELVE

When they reached what was left of the village, the fires were almost quenched. Bitter ash blew on the wind, stinging their faces as they gazed horror-stricken at the devastation before them. The only sound was the rain, as it spat and sputtered on embers.

"Who has done this?" cried David.

"Saxons," said Bear grimly.

Cai mouthed a curse.

The hunters split up. In ones and twos, they ran through the village calling for their families, desperately pushing aside still-smouldering timbers, dreading what they would find within. There were cries, wails, as the bodies of young and old were dragged from the ruins, and a few wretched survivors crept from the shelter of the forest. David's mind, camera-like, recorded an image of a burly young warrior weeping like a child, holding the body of his baby brother in his arms.

Bear, Cai, and Bedwyr ran for the chieftain's hall, with David panting behind them. On the way they passed Meri's hut, ruined and empty.

The hall showed evidence of a desperate struggle. The ground before it was drenched with blood and strewn with the bodies of the men and women who had tried to fight off the attackers. Their bodies lay sprawled where they had fallen, pitifully hacked and hewn, and stripped of their possessions. Right before the door lay Gwyladys, sword in hand, so covered with wounds that David could scarcely recognize her. The body of a huge Saxon warrior lay beside her, their blood pooling grotesquely.

Where was Meri?

The interior of the hall was badly damaged, though its sturdy frame had withstood the fire better than the flimsy huts in the village. It was wrecked, as if the invaders had sought to destroy what they couldn't carry away. Bodies lay everywhere. Seeing one man move feebly, Cai bent over him and shook him by the shoulder, none too gently.

"What happened? How long ago?"

The man, a warrior too old to follow Lord Rhodri's war band, tried to raise himself. Blood oozed from an ugly slash across the back of his head, and his face was bruised and swollen. Bear knelt at his side to lift him, while Bedwyr found an unbroken water jug in one corner and pressed a dripping ladle to the man's lips.

He swallowed, choked, then managed to gasp, "No more than an hour, I think. Saxons. Many of them. They came upriver in boats. Before we knew it, they were upon us!"

He gazed up at them, his eyes full of horror. "We tried to fight them off, to get as many of our people as we could to the hall and make a stand." He sobbed. "It was no use. They were too many. They overwhelmed us. Set fire to the hall. And they killed . . . they killed as if they loved doing it! Old women, children . . . "

"The filthy swine!" snarled Cai.

"Wait," said Bear urgently. "Prisoners. Did they take any?"

"Not many," mumbled the man. "Only the strongest children, and some of the women . . ."

"For slaves," finished Bedwyr, white-lipped.

"I saw your mother dragged from the hall, Lord Cai. And your betrothed. That Meri! She laid about her with a sword until they overpowered her. They took her little sister, too." His voice cracked. "The last few of us fought to save them, but one of those murderers must have taken me from behind with an axe. I don't remember any more." He began to weep again. "I'm ashamed to be alive! What will Lord Rhodri say . . ?"

Meri in the hands of those murderers! David felt sickness rising in the back of his throat. Cai, his face a mask of grief, swung around and plunged wildly out of the hall.

Bear tied a piece of rag around the wounded man's head and propped him up against the wall. "There," he said in a gentle voice, almost as if the grizzled old warrior were a child. "Rest now. You fought well. You all did. I see Saxon dead among our own."

He got to his feet and went out. Bedwyr followed. Sick at heart, David leaned against the doorway a moment. Then his eye was caught by a splash of mossy green against the muddy ground. A torn cloak, half-covering a crumpled body. A cloak he recognized. Slowly, David moved across the courtyard. It was

Branwyn, her skull split by an axe.

He fell to his knees, and time seemed to lurch around him. He saw the blood-smeared face before him, and yet another, too. Dead white against a hospital pillow.

"Mother . . ." he whispered. He dug the heels of his hands into his eyes. No, that was wrong. Wrong! That was another life. But this was just as bad. This was Branwyn. Kind Branwyn, who had nursed him so devotedly and tended everyone's hurts. She hadn't deserved to be butchered like this. Nobody did.

Time lurched again and he glimpsed battlefields, massacres, the killing grounds of his own time. Tears of pity and horror streamed down his face, springing from somewhere deep within him. He buried his face in his hands and wept.

Someone put a hand on his shoulder. It was Bear.

David tried to master his tears, but they kept flowing. "This is crazy," he sobbed, looking up at Bear. "Crazy! All this . . . this ugliness and death and . . . and hatred and cold-blooded murder. Can't someone stop the dying?"

Bear stared down at him for a long moment, his eyes widening as if in shock. Then, "I will," he said simply. He swung around, his back to the smouldering sunset, and pulled out his sword. He held it high, and a red gleam of fire from the dying sun ran down the naked blade. To David, still kneeling, he seemed to grow taller against the darkening sky.

"I WILL!" Bear shouted.

Will . . . will . . . will sang the echo from across the valley. People in the ruined village stopped where they were and turned to listen.

"Hear me!" Bear cried. "We're going after the murderers. AND WE'RE GOING TO GET OUR PEOPLE BACK!"

Back . . . back . . . back . . . mocked the echo.

A faint cheer rose from the grimy figures in the clearing. "Bear . . . Bear . . . Bear to lead us!" the young warriors cried, clashing their spears against their shields. The survivors added their ragged cheers.

David felt an electric charge shoot through him. He clambered to his feet.

Bear turned to Bedwyr, who had come on the run. "Find Cai quickly," he told him. "Tell him I need him down by the river."

Bear turned to David. "See what provisions you can gather, man. We can't leave the people here with nothing, but we can't move without supplies!" He limped toward the river, and Bedwyr and David raced off in opposite directions.

David began scouting the ruined huts for stores. Much had been taken by the raiders, and much spilled and trampled into the ground. At first, he felt as if he were robbing the dead. But then, seeing what he was about, the survivors began to help. They pressed around him, insisting he take a torn bag of flour, a muddied flitch of bacon.

"No, no, you must keep something for yourselves," he found himself protesting. And then, as the final argument, "Bear said so."

And the people nodded and obeyed. Men spoke gruff good wishes. Old women patted his shoulder and mumbled encouragement. David felt tears rise up again to choke his throat. He was one of them at last, accepted by them in their sorrow.

More quickly than he could have believed possible, he found himself at the riverbank with a pile of provisions. Bear and Bedwyr and Cai were surveying the boats. Most of them had been stove in by axe blows, but the warriors were making crude patches with oiled hides and hot pitch.

"Not very good, but they'll have to do. Boats are our only hope of catching up with them," said Bear, surveying the work critically. "Cai, you choose who should go with us. Pick only the best. I leave it to you. We'll see that the supplies are loaded."

Cai nodded. His arrogant bluster had deserted him, and he seemed glad enough to follow orders.

"He's blaming himself for what happened," said Bedwyr. "For taking us away on the hunt, you see."

"It's no more his fault than it is mine," said Bear. "I knew what was right. But I gave in to him. Because I wanted to go."

"You can't blame yourself!" David exclaimed.

"Can't I?" Bear asked bleakly.

"Well, you can, but you shouldn't," David shot back. "What good does it do?"

"David's right," said Bedwyr. "Happen we'd been here, we'd have put up a fight. Killed a few more of them. But the ending would have been the same. We couldn't have held off so many."

Bear shrugged. "Perhaps. But what matters now is to get our people back. Before . . ." He let his words trail off.

No one felt like asking how they would do it.

The boats were drawn up and supplies loaded. Cai returned at the head of a small group of warriors. "These are all the boats will hold," he said. "The others will stay to care for our folk. And see to the burying," he added grimly.

"Then let's go. Every minute counts," urged Bear. "Just pray that they make camp somewhere instead of travelling through the night. If not, we'll never catch them."

As they moved toward the boats, Cai rounded on David, his eyes blazing. "You never mean to take him along, do you?" he snarled at Bear. "Far better men than he have to stay behind. He'll be nothing but a burden to us."

David stopped in his tracks. It had never occurred to him that he wouldn't go with them. But Cai's right, he thought bitterly, I'd be no use to them. They're going into horrible danger. Maybe to their deaths. Why would I even want to go? I must be crazy!

Then Bear looked back over his shoulder and said, "What are you waiting for? You've surely learned by now not to listen to Cai's maundering, haven't you?"

To Cai he added, "He's no warrior, but he's clever and cannier than you know. We may need him. This is no ordinary battle we'll be fighting."

"Wait!" David spun on his heel and raced to Emrys's hut. His heart in his mouth, he ploughed through the tumbled mess inside to the corner where he had left Beauty. It was still there! He hesitated a moment. Beauty was not his to take. But Emrys was away and who knew how long it would be before he returned to the ruined village? He would not leave the harp behind. He slung it on his back and raced to the riverbank.

The other boats were pulling away, and only Bear's waited on the strand. Bear knelt on the muddy shore, Cabal's great rough head between his hands.

"I can't take you, boy. You're big as an ox, and would overturn us. Stay, Cabal. I'll be back." The big hound whined and sat down obediently. Bear stepped into the boat. David followed. Cai and Bedwyr pushed off, and they paddled out onto the rough black water.

Behind them, the village dwindled into a tiny island of light surrounded by darkness. Then a pitiful howl rose up into the night and quavered out across the water. It was Cabal, sorrowing and forsaken. David shivered, remembering those other, terrible Hounds. It sounded like the souls of the dead mourning for their lost lives. A moment later, the current seized them, and the village disappeared from sight around a bend.

The river, still swollen from spring rains, carried them swiftly. There was little need for them to do anything but steer. Just as well, David said to himself. If I had to man an oar now, I'd probably disgrace myself, and Cai would chuck me overboard!

They glided many miles downstream in total silence. Hours passed, and the moon rode high in a sky swept clear of clouds. Watching its light on the river and listening to the hiss of water against the boat, David nearly dozed off. He jerked awake when Bear sat up straighter and sniffed the wind like a hound. "Smoke again, though not much," he said in a low voice. "We'd better check the shore. Keep your voices down."

They signalled to the other boats to wait upstream against the shore, while their boat made for a glade near the edge of the river. There was no light to be seen, and no sound to be heard. Bear stepped ashore, motioning to the others to stay where they were. He melted into the darkness. Minutes later, he returned. "The remains of several fires, not long out," he said. "And this." He held out an object that glimmered in the dark.

It was a bracelet of twisted silver.

With a low cry of grief, Cai seized it. "Meri's!" he said dully. "I gave it her when we were betrothed."

He loves her too, David thought miserably. And then, Was it torn from her when . . . when . . .

"Nay, Cai, David," said Bear, glancing at their faces. "There's no need to think the worst. My eyes are keen even by moonlight, and I could see no signs of a struggle. I think they just came ashore to make a meal and left the prisoners tied up."

"But the bracelet?" faltered David.

Bear grinned wearily. "I think that's our Meri using her wits. She knows we'll follow, and she's letting us know that they were here, that they're all right so far. And, incidentally, that she's managed to loosen her bonds. That could be useful to know."

Cai looked up, his eyes kindling with hope. "I think you're right. That's exactly the kind of thing she'd think of!" He picked up his oar. "So what are we dallying here for?" he asked, with a touch of his old bravado. "They must have lost some time making a stop here. Let's be after them!"

Bear slapped him on the shoulder and clambered back into the boat.

Dawn found them far down the river. They raced between steep bluffs, which frowned down on them in the growing light. Then the valley broadened out and the river began to bend westward.

"They must be heading for Isca," muttered Bear, peering ahead. "We have to catch up with them before they get there."

"Why?" Bedwyr wanted to know.

"Walls, idiot," snapped Bear. Surprised at his tone, David glanced at him. Bear's face was ghastly pale, and the rough bandage around his wounded leg was clotted dark with blood.

He's exhausted, David thought. Running on sheer nerve.

As if recognizing his own sharpness, Bear spoke more gently. "We all know the Saxons aren't much at fighting in an organized way. But they're smart enough to hole up where there are fortifications they can take advantage of," he explained. "Once they're behind walls we'll have no chance at all of surprising them. And we can't fight them head-on like an army!"

"Then we've got to catch them first," growled Cai. "We've got to!"

THIRTEEN

The walls of the old Roman fort rose above a wide bend of the river. The rescue party pulled the boats ashore upstream and hid them well with brush and tree branches. Then they gathered around Bear, their faces grim.

"We lost the race," he said wearily. "Though if we had caught them out on the water there'd have been little we could do to stop them. They are many and have our people as hostages."

Cai, who had been up the hill to scout, spoke up. "Looks to me as if they're planning to stay in the fort for now," he said. "The boats are pulled well up along the shore, and I can see smoke from fires inside the walls."

Bear nodded. "There are probably other parties out raiding the countryside," he said. "They must have a large ship down on the Hafren. To carry off their booty to the Saxon Shore."

"And their slaves," added Bedwyr sombrely.

A murmur of agreement ran around the circle of tired faces.

"Somehow some of us have to get into the fort," Bear went on. "It won't be easy. The walls won't be in good repair, but the Saxons aren't fools. They'll have posted guards. But if we can get a few of us inside without the Saxons' knowing, we can take out the guards and warn our people to be ready. Then the rest of us can risk a surprise attack."

"But how do we do that?" someone asked.

"We can't do much until dark. Let me think on it," said Bear. "Meanwhile, let's eat something and get some rest. Bedwyr . . ?" His voice trailed off hopefully."

"I'll see to the food," said Bedwyr. "Some of you help me with the supplies."

The others drifted off to search for firewood.

"Dry wood, and only a little," Bear called after them. "We can't afford to show smoke." He sank down on a mossy log, his wounded leg held out stiffly before him. It was an ugly sight, the bandage now filthy and crusted black with blood.

David swallowed, hard, then, "Let me have a look at that," he offered. Unslinging Beauty, he knelt down and began peeling off the dirty bandage.

Bear drew in his breath with a pained hiss. "Minstrel you may be, but you surely haven't a healer's hands," he complained, as David laid the wound bare.

Looking at the gaping tear in Bear's leg, David swallowed. "It's a mess," he said frankly. "Back where I come from you'd be whisked off to hospital for stitches and an antibiotic shot in your rear."

"Eh?" Bear looked down at him, puzzled.

"We spoke of it once. Don't you remember? Needles full of powerful medicine that doctors stick into you?"

Bear grinned through his pain. "I don't feel as if I

need anything else stuck into me right now, happen we did have such a thing. If you'll just do your best to clean up the wound and bind it, I'd be grateful."

David fetched water upstream of the camp to wash the wound. Then he rummaged around in the supplies for a fairly clean piece of sacking and cut strips of it with his dagger to bandage the leg tightly. Still kneeling, he looked up at Bear. "It's stopped bleeding, and it's fairly clean now. But I don't know herbs or anything to put on it for healing, or to help with the pain . . . " Suddenly he thought of Branwyn, and his eyes misted over. He looked down quickly.

"It will do. Thanks," said Bear.

His voice was oddly gentle, and David guessed that his thoughts were the same as his own. "What are we going to do, Bear?" he asked, looking up again.

"I don't know yet," Bear confessed, his eyes troubled. "We need to get someone inside. But how?" He shook his head. "Unless we can do that, we haven't a prayer of getting enough warriors in to help our people. The raiders will carry the prisoners off to the Saxon lands as thralls. It will be the last we'll see of any of them."

David felt black misery settle over him. Meri was right there inside those walls. Maybe she hadn't been harmed yet. But she would be. They had to help her. And Lady Eluned and the rest. But what if Bear couldn't think of a way?

Much good his past and future knowledge did him now, he thought. He'd never learned much about wars. Now he was in the middle of one. His thoughts went round in a circle. Meri. The walls. Themselves on the outside. They needed to get inside, but weren't strong enough to fight their way in. Somehow it reminded him of a story he knew. An old story . . .

"What we need is a wooden horse," he said, half to himself.

"A what?" Bear wasn't paying attention.

"Oh, nothing. Nothing useful. Just something out of an old tale . . ."

Bear was all attention now."Let me be the judge of that. Tell me!" he demanded.

David began, "Long ago people called Greeks laid siege to a city named Troy. I forget why, exactly. Anyway it doesn't matter. But these Greeks, see, they had the same problem we've got. The city had strong walls and many warriors inside. The Greeks couldn't fight their way in."

"So?"

"So they decided to get in by trickery. They built this wooden horse. A big one. And they put some of their warriors inside. Then they left the horse outside the city gates and pretended to go away."

"And what happened?" Bear's eyes were riveted on David's.

"Well, the Trojans thought the Greeks had given up and left the horse as some kind of tribute. So they pulled the horse inside the city walls. And later, while the Trojans were celebrating their victory, the Greek soldiers came out of the horse and opened the gates for the rest of the army. And that was the end of Troy!"

For a long moment, Bear said nothing. David began to feel foolish. What use was it to tell the story anyway?

It didn't solve their problem.

"Sorry. I guess it's a pretty dumb idea," he said lamely. "I know you can't come up with a wooden horse . . ."

Bear jumped to his feet, his eyes blazing. "No, but a live horse, perhaps. And a cart. And tribute, of a kind."

"You mean you've actually thought of something?" David stared at him in amazement.

Bear laughed wildly. "*You* thought of it. But I think I know how to make it work for us. Come on!" He strode off toward the others, his weariness and pain forgotten.

Bear's plan was simple. They would scour the nearby farms for a cart of some kind and a horse or pony to pull it. They'd load into it as many goods as they could find. And at dusk, someone would drive it right past the old Roman fort.

"The Saxons will never be able to resist seizing it and taking it inside. Never!" Bear crowed. "And if we're lucky, they'll be too busy with the contents to look underneath the cart, where some of us will be concealed. Once the Saxons have taken the bait, we can sneak out and deal with the guards, maybe even unbar the gates for the rest of us."

"It could work!" Cai said, his eyes alight. "Any road, it's the only chance we've got!"

"Are we agreed, then?" asked Bear, glancing around the circle of eager faces. There was a murmur of assent. "Then let's get on with it. We haven't much time."

They split into groups. Cai would lead one scavenging party, and Bedwyr another. Bear and David would make a third.

"There's a small settlement not far away, and farms

are scattered all around this area," Bear told them. "Some will have been picked clean by the Saxons. But I'm hoping the raiders haven't had time to find all there is to find."

"What if some of the farmers are still about?" someone asked.

"Then you'll have to persuade them to give us what we need," replied Bear. "Do try to be nice about it, won't you?" he added, dryly. Everybody laughed. "Now let's go! Try to be back in no more than a couple of hours. We must make our move before it's too dark."

Half an hour later, David found himself peering out from under a particularly thorny gorse bush on the edge of a farmyard about a kilometre from the river.

"It seems quiet," said Bear in a low voice. Then, looking at the dilapidated hut and barn, he added, "What a benighted little cot! Phew! did you ever smell a riper dung heap?"

He drew his sword and edged cautiously toward the house, with David at his heels. The door of the hut gaped open. Inside, they found evidence of hasty flight. Bins and boxes stood open, as if provisions had been hastily collected. But there was no sign of looting.

"Must have heard about the raiders and gone off somewhere safer," said Bear. "Let's see what they've left behind for us."

It wasn't much. A sack half full of lentils and a string of onions were all they could find.

"Let's hope we have better luck in the barn," commented Bear, looking disgusted. The barnyard was empty, save for a couple of miserable-looking hens.

David chased the squawking fowl and stuffed them into a sack. By the time he had caught them he was out of breath and out of temper. "No luck, I suppose," he said crossly as Bear came back from the barn empty-handed.

Bear shook his head, looking grim. "They took the horses. Too valuable to leave behind. Let's hope the others find something that can pull a cart. If not . . ."

Just then, a strange sound came from behind the barn. Something between a loud wheeze and a klaxon horn. David spun around. "What was that?" he asked nervously, as the sound came again.

Bear was grinning. "Maybe, just maybe, the answer to our problem." He disappeared into the barn and came out in a moment with a bridle. Then the two of them circled the building. There, in a kind of rough paddock, stood a large dusty-grey beast with long ears.

David was puzzled. "What is it?" he asked. "It's too big for a donkey. And pretty weird-looking for a horse."

"Mule," said Bear. He clambered over the fence and walked slowly toward the animal. "A nice mule, a very, very nice mule," he went on, coaxingly. "Aren't you, old fellow?"

The mule pricked its ears forward. It let Bear approach to within an arm's length, then trotted a short distance away. Bear tried again and again, but each time the same thing happened.

"Wretched brute!" Bear said feelingly. "No wonder they left it behind for the Saxons."

"Maybe you should try bribing him," said David, tossing Bear an onion from the string slung over his shoulder.

Bear shrugged and held out the onion on the palm of his hand. Step by step, the beast came closer, stretching out its ungainly muzzle. As it took the onion and began to crunch it, Bear threw the bridle over its head and made it fast. Then, as the mule tried to back away, he leaped onto its back and clung there. Snorting and braying, the mule began to buck.

"Yeeee-ha!" whooped David, doubled over with laughter. "Ride 'em, cowboy!"

Still clinging to the mule's back, Bear grabbed one of its long ears. He pulled it back and sank his teeth into it. The mule gave an astonished bray, then stood quite still.

"That's amazing," gasped David, tears of laughter still running down his face.

Grimacing, Bear slid down off the mule's back. "An old horseman's trick. And the brute deserves it. He's made my leg bleed again," he said. He shifted the rough bit of wattle fence that served as a gate and led the mule out of the paddock.

Back at the camp, they found Cai and his group had arrived, pulling a battered-looking cart loaded with supplies.

"I never thought to find myself playing cart-horse," grumbled Cai. "I'm glad to see that mule!"

"Let's get some straps rigged under the cart," said Bear. "If we're clever, there should be room for two of us to hang on under there."

"Come on, Onion," David said, leading the mule over to a rich patch of grass and tethering him to a bush. "Eat up. You've got an exciting night ahead of you." He went back to stand behind Bear. "And speaking of excitement," he began, "who . . ."

He broke off as Bedwyr and his group straggled in rolling two large oaken kegs before them.

"What on earth . . . !" began Cai.

Bedwyr, clearly delighted with himself, was grinning from ear to ear. "The village was deserted. But guess what we found in the head-man's hut—mead!"

"Good man!" exclaimed Bear, clapping him on the shoulder. "The Saxons won't bother lugging that all the way back to their ship. They're sure to drink every drop. All the better for us!"

"I wouldn't mind a mouthful of it myself," muttered Cai, as he turned back to fastening the straps under the cart. "A pity to waste it on Saxons."

Bear glanced at David. "You were asking . . . ?"

David nodded. "Who goes with the cart? Will we draw lots?"

Bear shook his head. "Nay, David. The warriors won't follow just anybody. If not me, then Cai must be the one to lead them. Besides, he's too large to fit under the cart. Bedwyr and I are smaller and quicker on our feet. We'll be the ones to go."

"But who drives the cart?" asked David. His mouth felt strangely dry as he asked.

Bear's eyes met his squarely. "That's the most dangerous job of all. Because the Saxons probably won't bother making a prisoner of the driver. If he can't talk his way around them, they're likely to just kill him outright. And if they don't kill him, and our attack fails, the rest of us will die quickly. But the driver will wear a Saxon slave collar for the rest of his days!"

David stood silent for a moment, thinking of Meri. Then, as if from a great distance, he heard himself saying words he hadn't thought he could bring himself to utter. "Well, I'm not up on my Saxon. But if you're looking for someone totally harmless, who better than a wandering minstrel?"

As he spoke, an owl hooted from somewhere in the darkening woods behind them.

FOURTEEN

L et's go," said Bear. With a grunt of discomfort, he swung himself under the cart, slipping his body through the loops attached under both ends of it.

"Mind your leg, man. Can you manage?" asked Bedwyr, exchanging a glance with David.

"I'll have to, won't I?" came the muffled response. Then, "Hurry up, the two of you. The less time I have to spend hanging here like a trussed fowl, the happier I'll be."

Bedwyr swung himself under the far side of the cart, and David clambered onto the top.

The light was fading fast, and the wind was rising. He could hear it soughing overhead in the branches. The owl called again, closer this time. The hair rose on the back of his neck. Was it Blodeuwedd?

Bear's pained voice came from under the wagon. "Get a move on, for pity's sake. And if that wretched mule balks, bite him again!"

I wonder how you put a mule in gear? David puzzled to himself. He gave the animal's rump a smart slap with the reins. "C'mon, Onion. Giddap," he said loudly. To his astonishment, the mule obeyed, and the heavily-laden cart jolted out onto the rutted road

The dark bulk of the fort loomed not far ahead of him. He peered into the gathering dusk looking for some sign of Cai and the rest. They should be hidden near the fort by now.

What was Cai thinking about, out there in the darkness?

The red-haired warrior had spoken to him before the two groups separated. "Bear told me it was you that first thought of the ruse," he said gruffly. "And that you volunteered to drive the cart. He paused for a moment, then went on, biting off the words as if he found them hard to say. "I'm grateful. Even if . . . I saw you and Meri in the woods that day, you know. I hadn't liked you before, but after that I hated you. Because I was afraid of losing her. Now, who knows? It may be too late for Meri, my mother, all of them. And us."

"I'm no warrior, as you've proved often enough," said David. "But you'll find a way to save them. You and Bear and Bedwyr."

With a half-embarrassed nod, Cai had turned away.

Wherever Cai is now, he won't be nervous, David thought. Cai didn't have a nerve in his body. He himself was so frightened he was almost numb. What if he botched things somehow, and the others never had a chance to carry out the rescue?

Let me do this right, he prayed. Please. For Meri.

To keep his spirits up, he began to sing. After all, the whole point now was to get himself noticed. Too bad he couldn't play Beauty and drive the cart at the same time.

He began with the first thing that came into his head.

One hundred bottles of mead on the wall,
One hundred bottles of mead.
What have you got when you take one away?
Ninety-nine bottles of mead!

His voice came out strained and wobbly, but after a few choruses he controlled it. "Sorry for the quality of the entertainment!" he called down to the others. "Ninety-six bottles of mead on the wall . . ."

He had worked his way through "Row, Row, Row Your Boat" and "Hi-ho, Hi-ho!" before the action started. By this time, one wall of the fort was not far away, and over the creaking of the cart he heard shouting. Torches flared along the top of the walls, and then a lighted gap appeared. The Saxons must have opened a gate!

He was just level with the fort when they came down on him, moving with amazing speed for such huge men. In less than a minute, they had surrounded him and seized the mule's head. David was jerked off the cart and dumped on the ground. He found himself looking up at a circle of ferocious faces wreathed in straggly blond hair and huge drooping moustaches. Seen from that angle, the Saxons looked at least ten feet tall.

One of them, who was, if possible, even larger than the rest, growled a question and prodded David painfully in the ribs with the edge of a wicked-looking battle axe.

"Ouch! Hi!" David stammered. "Uh, no harm

intended, fellows. I'm just passing through. To market, to market, y'know . . ."

The question was repeated, and the axe dug into his ribs again.

Too scared to say anything more, David simply held up both hands to show he was unarmed. He hoped they wouldn't think to search him and find the dagger he had tucked into his leggings.

The blond giant reached down and picked him up by the neck of his tunic. David found himself dangling in mid-air, his feet at least half a metre off the ground. The Saxon shook him as a terrier shakes a rat, then, with a nasty smile, he laid the blade of the axe against David's jugular.

The cold metal bit into his neck. David closed his eyes and braced himself for the final agonizing slash.

Just then a pleased-sounding growl went around the group who were investigating the cart. They had found the mead. The giant dropped David and strode over to join them. They pawed through the rest of the things in the cart, and a loud argument broke out. The giant cut it short with one bellowed word of command and a sharp gesture in the direction of the fort.

Thaaat's right, you big, dumb ox, thought David, holding his breath. Take it inside. Don't bother to look at it too closely.

One of the warriors took hold of Onion's bridle and tried to lead him. The mule refused to budge.

"Please, be a good mule," said David, reaching out a hand to pat the beast's muzzle. "Don't balk now." Either his words or a hard smack on the rump from one of the Saxons convinced Onion. He trotted up the track to the fort.

The remaining Saxons turned back to David. Uh-oh, he thought, now I'm for it! His stomach heaved, but there wasn't enough in it to throw up. They closed around him grinning wolfishly. Then the leader held something up. It was Beauty. He pointed to David, then to the harp and asked a question. The meaning was clear.

David nodded. "Yes. It's mine. I play it."

The Saxon's grin widened. He handed the harp to David and said something to the others, who laughed in agreement. Then he prodded David with the axe, and jerked his thumb in the direction of the fort.

David drew a deep breath. They weren't going to kill him, then. At least, not yet. Relief swept over him, and suddenly his knees began to tremble. He stumbled and nearly fell flat on his face on the muddy path. The Saxon prodded him onward, none too gently.

Seen close up, the fort was in much poorer repair than it had seemed from a distance. Its timber and stone walls were falling apart, and large gaps had opened up here and there. The buildings attached to the walls were even more dilapidated. The Saxons passed through an inner gate and into a larger compound where fires had been lit and spitted carcasses set to roast above the flames. David looked around for the captives, but at first could see no sign of them. Then he made out a small group huddled in a corner away from the fires. Was Meri among them, or was she . . . had they . . ?

The Saxons unloaded the cart and drove it to the far side of the compound. They had already broached one of the kegs of mead. David tried to locate the sentries, and made out at least four. Somehow, Bear and Bedwyr would have to disable some of them so that Cai and the rest could get into the fort. It was up to him to provide a distraction so they could slip from under the cart.

His heart in his mouth, he swept a crashing chord across the harp and stepped into the firelight. Then he bowed. "How about a little dinner music, you filthy murdering brutes?" he asked pleasantly.

The Saxons gazed at him open-mouthed, and for an awful moment, David wondered if they had somehow understood what he had said. One or two of them reached for their axes, but the leader roared out an order and signalled David to go on.

David bowed again and started singing. He began with battle chants, guessing that although they wouldn't know the words they'd get the spirit of the thing. Heads nodded and the mead went round. David noticed that horns of it were being carried to the sentries. Good.

Deciding that the meat was well-enough charred, the men began to carve off great hunks of it with their daggers. They crammed greasy slabs of it into their mouths and washed them down with gulps of mead.

An hour passed. Locked inside the ring of firelight, David couldn't see if Bear and Bedwyr had disentangled themselves from the cart. He had to keep on singing as long as he could. On he went. Ballads, love songs, it all seemed the same to the Saxons.

On impulse, he decided to toss in an old Led Zeppelin number. It sounded pretty weird on the harp, but nobody seemed to mind. Then he tried Deep Purple.

The Who. Pearl Jam. The Saxons ate it up.

One of them even reeled over and offered him a swig from his greasy drinking horn. Afraid to refuse, David took a mouthful and nearly spat it out. It was strong and rank and sickeningly sweet.

"Hey, you guys are a dream audience, y'know what I mean?" David said to the Saxon, wiping his mouth. "I mean totally out to lunch!"

The Saxon roared with laughter and slapped him so hard on the shoulder that he nearly fell down.

Luckily, the leader bawled an order and David's admirer staggered back to the fireside.

On and on David sang. The second keg of mead was broached and drunk, and here and there warriors rolled over snoring. The leader, however, stayed alert. At last, he got up and shoved David in the direction of the other captives.

"Party's over, is it?" asked David huskily, his voice almost gone. "Good time had by all, I hope?"

The Saxon gestured for him to put down the harp. He bound David's wrists and ankles tightly with leather thongs, then kicked his feet out from under him, so that he fell heavily to the ground.

"Always a critic in the crowd," muttered David to his retreating back.

He rolled over and raised his head to look at the others, who lay nearby wrapped in their cloaks. "Meri? Lady Eluned?" he whispered hoarsely.

Then Meri's voice came softly to him through the darkness. "David! I knew it was your voice. Oh, they've taken you too!"

He inched himself closer. "Meri, I'm not alone," he whispered. "Bear, Cai and the others are here. . . We're going to set you free."

"But that's impossible!"

"Never mind. We found the bracelet you dropped. Are your hands still free?"

"Yes. I managed to work the knot loose."

"Then see if you can find my right legging. I've hidden a dagger."

He heard her sliding stealthily over to him. She touched the side of his face for a moment, then fumbled with the legging.

"I've got it!" she breathed.

"Cut my bonds, then the others'. Tell them to be ready to run. And you keep the knife. In case . . ."

He heard her draw in her breath. Then, "Yes," she said steadily. "That would be best."

He rolled onto his stomach and raised his wrists. In a moment he felt the knife slice through the thong that bound them, and his ankles were freed too. Then Meri, crawling on her stomach, moved away to the others. Moments later, someone else moved close beside him, and hands clutched at his sleeve.

"David?" The small voice sounded choked with tears.

"Hush, Arianrod," he whispered. "Not so loud. You don't want the nasties to hear you!"

She huddled closer. "I hate them," she muttered. "They killed everyone. And they beat us, too. Because we tried to fight them."

He put an arm tightly around her. "Shhh. I know. Be quiet now."

She fell silent. He heard a muffled thud. Were Bear and Bedwyr about their work? He looked hastily back at the fires. They had burned down, and even the leader had rolled himself in his cloak and lain down beside the others.

A shadow detached itself from the corner of the wall and flitted noiselessly over to them. "Any time now," Bear hissed in his ear. "Don't let our folk head for the main gate. The Saxons will expect that. Lead them out past the corner of that shed. There's a gap in the wall."

"Unguarded?" asked David.

He saw the flash of white teeth as Bear grinned. "It is now," he said. Then he was gone into the darkness.

As if from nowhere, lighted torches sailed over the wall, setting the roofs of the sheds alight. Black figures shouting battle cries poured through gaps in the walls, and spears whined into the group of sleeping men around the fire. There were shouts of pain and confusion, as the Saxons seized their weapons. David spied Bear in the thick of the fight, hewing left and right with his sword. Cai, his ruddy hair backlit by the flames, was attacking two confused Saxons at once.

And suddenly, David was back in his old nightmare. The leaping flames, the running figures, the screams, the noise. It was the scene he'd been dreaming all his life. He froze. But how could he have a memory of this? Dazed, he passed a hand over his eyes.

Then Meri's voice pierced his numbness. "Let's get everybody out!" she shouted. "Help Eluned. She's hurt."

"This way," David shouted back, springing to life. "Not the gate!" Half-carrying Lady Eluned, he led them past the shed Bear had pointed out. It was on fire, and just as they passed it, the roof collapsed in a shower of sparks. Around it, and past, and there was the gap. He heard shouts close behind them and whirled. A Saxon warrior was bearing down on them, sword raised.

"Arianrod," David cried, turning back, "lead the others through. Head for the woods!"

She nodded and scampered through. David passed Eluned through the gap to two of the boys and realized Meri wasn't behind him.

He turned to face the Saxon. Then, "Meri, no!" he screamed.

She was face to face with the warrior. Slightly crouched, she was circling him, dagger in hand. Almost lazily, he struck at her with his axe, and blood poured down from her shoulder. Even so, she sprang forward and slashed him with the dagger, then danced back out of reach. With a roar of rage, he bore down on her, raising the axe.

David looked around frantically for a weapon. He seized a smouldering timber, and with a strength he'd never known he possessed, he rushed forward and swung at the Saxon's legs, catching him behind the knees. The warrior's legs buckled, and he staggered forward. Quick as a cat, Meri leapt around him and sank the dagger into his back. As he groaned and tried to turn, she jerked the blade out and stabbed him again. He collapsed and lay still.

Meri stood over the body gasping and trembling, still holding the bloody dagger. She looked at it, then at David, and tears rolled down her cheeks. "I've never . . .

But I had to . . . Oh, David!" she said.

"Let's get out of here," shouted David. Seizing her by the wrist, he dragged her to the gap in the wall and shoved her through. He was about to follow himself when he remembered.

Beauty! He'd left the harp behind.

"Go on to the others. They're in the woods!" he shouted to Meri. Then he turned and raced back into his nightmare.

Always, when he had dreamed it, he'd known he was looking for something. Something precious, something he had to find. But the flames and smoke and darkness of the dream had always hidden it from him. And when he'd awakened, he could never remember what it was he had looked for so desperately. Now he knew.

The whole fort was ablaze around him, as the timbers in the walls caught fire from the burning sheds. The figures of fighting warriors were silhouetted against the flames. At this distance, he couldn't tell who was who, or who was winning. Bear and the others would have to get out soon. They were too few to hold the Saxons for long.

At last, he found the corner. Beauty lay where he had left it, its golden wood reflecting the flames all around. He seized it with a sob of relief. Clutching it, he raced back toward the wall. A figure loomed up ahead of him in the smoke, and he couldn't see whether it was friend or foe. Then another roof collapsed with a roar, and a hot gust of air tore a rent in the smoke. David found himself face to face with the Saxon leader.

There wasn't even time to be afraid. He saw the gleam

of a red sword descending and felt a stunning blow. As he fell, his hand, still clutching Beauty, tore the strings asunder in one last dissonant chord. He spun down into darkness.

FIFTEEN

Light. Light so bright it hurt his eyes. A faint murmur of voices. And somewhere an odd mechanical beep. He let his eyelids close and sank back into the dark.

It was night when he awoke again. The light was dimmer, and this time he managed to keep his eyes open. His head hurt. Funny, he thought he'd got over that long ago. Branwyn's draughts . . . His left leg throbbed fiercely, too. It seemed to be tied up on some kind of pulley. And his left arm was fastened to some kind of board. There was a needle stuck in it, with a tube leading out. He shifted his head slightly. Behind him was a bank of instruments, monitor lights blinking red and green . . . That didn't make sense.

"Bear! Bedwyr!" he called. Had they got away? Was Meri safe with the others? He tried to sit up, but found he couldn't move.

"None of that now." A head crowned with a white cap shaped like a muffin popped up over the side of the bed. Wide brown eyes looked down. "You've been out for quite a while, lad. Had us all worried, you did."

He squinted as she came into focus. She was small, round as a ball, and her nose was as speckled with freckles as a plover's egg. At first, he thought she was very young, but then he noticed tiny laugh lines around her eyes and mouth, and threads of grey in her brown hair.

She gave him a crooked grin. "What an expression! I'm not that bad to look at, surely?" she joked.

"No, I . . ." He looked around desperately. "It's just that I don't remember . . ."

"Where you are? In Caerleon, now. Though that's not where they found you, I'm told. Somewhere away up-country it was. Some daft stunt with a motorcycle."

"It can't be! I was here, or at least near here! I was. . . " He paused, then asked, "What date is it, nurse?"

She raised her eyebrows. "March 28. You needn't ask the year. You haven't been out that long!" she added, and grinned again. "And you can call me Puddy. That's my name."

"March 28? Puddy? That's a funny name," said David woozily.

"It's Welsh, young man, and I'm proud of it," she snapped. Then she added, "Now stop thrashing about. If you pull out the drip needle, Matron will have a fit. Anyone would think you weren't glad to be awake again!"

David lay still, his thoughts racing.

"I'm turning the lights down. Now you just try to rest until morning, do you hear?" she went on. "I'll be phoning your father. Poor man, it's relieved he'll be. He's been here night and day, you know, until we made him go home to rest. We didn't need the two of you to look after!"

The light grew dimmer. David closed his eyes. He was back, then. But she'd said March 28. That was only a week or so after the day he'd gone off. But months had passed in Prydein! It had been early summer when the Saxons had attacked, and they had set off on their mad pursuit.

Nobody will believe me. The thought made the bottom drop out of his stomach. They'll say I was just dreaming. Or that I'm crazy.

But I'm not crazy. I'm not! And it wasn't just a dream. Couldn't be! I've never dreamed anything like that before . . .

Haven't you? It was almost as though another voice spoke inside him. What about your old nightmare? The flames, the figures running. You dreamed that, didn't you? For years and years. And now you know where it came from. It's all part of the same story. You've just gotten crazier. Even the pain you felt there was no more than the echo of your pain here. It was none of it real, you dreamed all of it.

"No!" he shouted. "No! I couldn't have! Not Meri. Not Bear!"

"I thought I told you to rest!" Puddy was back at his bedside. "We can't have you disturbing the other patients," she told him crossly. "If you can't sleep, we'll give you a nice big jab of something to make you. Is that what you want?"

"No," whispered David. "No. I'll try to sleep."

"See that you do," she said. But she placed a cool hand on his forehead for a moment before she left him.

His father came in the morning. David saw that his

141

face was lined with fatigue, his eyes rimmed with dark shadows. It was like looking at a stranger. For a long moment, they eyed each other warily.

Then David began, "I know, I know. You don't have to tell me. I've really done it this time . . ."

"No, wait. There's something I have to say." His father's words cut sharply across his. "I'd . . . I'd better say it now before everything . . . goes wrong between us again," he added. He turned toward the window for a moment, as though looking for a way out, then turned back. "I blame myself for what happened. The quarrel, I mean. Maybe even the accident. I pushed you too hard. I guess that's a bad habit of mine."

He pulled a chair closer to the side of the bed. Sat down, leaned forward. "I've had plenty of time to think, this last week. Not knowing whether you'd ever wake up. Or whether, if you did, it would be with your mind . . . damaged." He paused, then went on with a rush. "So I just want to say that you don't have to stay with me. I guess it was a crazy idea all along. Anyway, I was wrong to force you to come with me, to leave what you wanted to do for what I wanted to do. I have to stay, of course, until the end of the school year. But you can go back as soon as you're well enough. I've called your aunt Laura, and she'll put you up. Then, when I come back, maybe we can work out what to do about the future."

Leave! The thought made David dizzy. "I don't want . . . I might want to stay," he said.

"You don't have to say that," his father began.

"I'm not thinking about you," said David. "Not really. I just . . . I need time to sort some things out.

And it might be easier here."

Puddy appeared and tapped her watch meaningfully. "You weren't supposed to stay long this first time, Mr. Baird. And you weren't supposed to do so much talking," she said sternly. "Now, you do remember, you promised. Matron is quite strict . . ."

"Sorry. I guess I got carried away." David's father stood up awkwardly and went to the door. "Try to rest," he said, looking back. "I'll come when they'll let me."

David nodded.

"Now," said the little nurse. She cocked her head and stood looking down at him, arms akimbo. "Bath time, is it?"

"Oh, cripes," said David.

The days soon fell into a dreary routine. He couldn't leave the hospital until his leg, which was badly broken, was out of traction. He couldn't even leave his bed. It was bad enough to be at the mercy of a bossy nurse, he told himself. But to have to use a bedpan and have her wipe his bottom!

Even worse was his brooding about what had happened. As the days passed his mood grew blacker. Part of him believed it had all been a dream. Stupid bloody fool, he told himself, why keep mooning over people who never really existed?

But another part of him wept for the loss of Meri. And Bear and Bedwyr. They had seemed so real. They had to be real!

He grew surly, and snapped at his father and Puddy.

His father bit back angry words and put up with his bad temper. Puddy gave back as good as she got. "The way you speak to your father is a scandal," she scolded David after one visit. "And him trying to be so nice to you and all."

David scrunched down on his pillows and avoided her accusing gaze. "What do you know about it, anyway?" he mumbled.

"Oh, I know the two of you have problems. And probably not all your fault. That's clear enough," she said sternly. "But still and all, that's water under the bridge, isn't it? You have to go on from here, somehow. What else can you do?"

"I'm not over-nice to you either, am I?" he said, looking at her out of the corner of his eye.

"Not especially. But it goes with the job, doesn't it?" she snapped. And bustled off, with a crackle of starched apron.

They did some tests, not very nice ones, to make sure his brain hadn't been damaged.

"Though I told them there was nothing wrong with you but black temper," said Puddy. "And that wouldn't show up on any test!"

Still David couldn't eat. Slept poorly. Puddy was on the night shift again, and he often roused from a fitful doze to find her beside his bed.

"Haven't you got any other patients to pester?" he snapped at her one night.

"None like you. You're weird, you are," she said tartly. "Did you know that you cry in your sleep?"

David brushed the back of his free hand across his cheek. It was wet.

"You'd better pull yourself together, my lad," she said

frankly. "I shouldn't tell you this, but they're thinking of sending in a psychiatrist to find out what's bothering you."

"A shrink?" David was fully awake now. "I won't talk to him. I just . . . can't."

There was a long pause. Then, "I guess I do need to talk to someone, though," he admitted. "I can't keep going over it all in my head."

Somewhere a distant church bell chimed three. "Could you talk to me?" asked Puddy. "My ward is quiet this time of night."

"You'll think I'm crazy," said David.

"Make a nice change from nasty, that will," she shot back, sitting down beside the bed.

So he told her all of it. Slowly, hesitantly, at first, then faster and faster, stumbling over his words as he tried to make her understand what had happened, how it had been.

"And I went back for the harp," he finished. "That was when it happened. A sword . . . And then I woke up here." He looked across at her, bracing himself for her disbelief.

But Puddy's eyes were shining, and her cheeks were flushed. "That's . . . that's the most wonderful tale I've ever heard," she said softly. "It's like a romance, isn't it? Meri and all. But that Bear! There was something special about him, there was. Ah, that's the kind of lad to make a girl's heart beat faster!"

"You talk about them as if they were real," said David cautiously. "Not . . . just some sick fantasy."

"But there is something real about it all, isn't there?

I mean, it wasn't like a normal sort of a dream." Puddy sighed, then added, "Though I suppose it must be. But oh, I wish I could dream like that."

"I can't bear it to be a dream," said David miserably. "That's what's been eating me all this time. I miss them. There's nothing here for me that means as much as they do."

Puddy got up and smoothed the sheet across his chest. "But there were bad things, ugly things there too," she said.

David sighed. "Yes. But the world seemed so clean and green. And people were easier to understand, somehow. Even the ones I didn't like. And in the end they accepted me."

She thought for a moment. "I'm no psychiatrist, but I think that if you could cope with all that you can surely find a way to manage here," she replied. "Maybe that's what your mind is trying to tell you."

"I guess," he said, trying to smile. "But oh, Puddy, I'm so lonely. I feel . . . different, as if I've changed, somehow. Nothing seems to fit anymore."

She went over to the window and twitched back the curtain. "Nearly dawn," she said. "You must try to rest. Matron will skin me if she finds out I let you lie awake so long." But she lingered for a moment, biting her lip, then went on, "Do you know, though, there's someone else you could tell this to."

"The shrink?" countered David.

"Certainly, if you want to. But no, I was thinking of an uncle of mine. He was some great boffin at the university until he retired. Knows all about Welsh history and such.

I'll give you his address, if you like. He lives over Cardiff way. You could go see him when you get out of this place. You might feel less lonely talking about it with someone who knows about that kind of thing."

"Maybe I will," said David, closing his eyes again. "And, Puddy . . . thanks!"

SIXTEEN

The man at the door of the cottage was not at all what David expected. He had pictured a retired professor as someone wizened, tall and thin, bald maybe, and definitely severe. Professor Geraint Davies was tiny, like Puddy. But where she was plump, he was slender. He didn't even look particularly old, though his dark hair was thickly streaked with silver. His heavy brows were dark, as were the sharp eyes below them. David thought he looked a bit like an elf.

"Come in, come in," he said, smiling. "I'm Geraint Davies. You'll be David Baird, then. My niece has been telling me about you."

"I'll bet," said David. His crutches thumped on the polished floor as he followed the professor through the hall into a tiny living room. "What did she say—that I was her most troublesome patient ever, and daft into the bargain?"

"Not exactly, but she warned me you'd probably say something like that about yourself. Let me take your jacket." He glanced down at the heavy cast on David's leg. "It must be awkward getting about with that on," he said. "Does your leg still pain you much?"

"A bit," David admitted. "But it's great to be out of traction. And out of the hospital."

"Sit down and be comfortable." The professor pointed to a worn armchair that looked ready to burst at the seams. He picked up a poker and tried to stir up a small, messy fire smouldering in the grate. "Now, then," he said, turning around, "I was about to have tea. Will you join me? Or, let me see. You're Canadian, aren't you? Perhaps you don't like tea. I'm not quite sure what else I can offer you. I haven't any —what is that odd word you call minerals over there—pop?"

"Tea's okay," said David, who didn't really like it much.

He sat looking about the room while Professor Davies clattered about in the kitchen. Books were piled everywhere, and there was a strong smell of pipe tobacco in the air. Some kind of old map, framed, hung over the fireplace. There was a music stand in one corner with a flute propped against a page of music.

"Here we are." The professor bustled back with a laden tray, which he set on a low table before the fire. He sat down opposite David and lifted the chipped brown teapot. "Will you take milk and sugar? I recommend plenty of both. I make my tea fierce."

"That'll be fine," said David.

"And do try the seedcake," Professor Davies added. "Made with real Welsh butter, of course. I make it myself. It's my one domestic skill. And if I do say so, you'll never taste better."

David took a bite of the cake, which was rich with butter and tasted of caraway seed. Clever one, he is, he thought to himself, chewing. Rambling on like this, letting me get used to the situation. I wonder how much Puddy told him? He took a sip of his tea. It wasn't so bad. The sugar helped a lot.

"So then," said the professor, setting down his cup and leaning back comfortably, "I hear you have a story to tell me." He tented his long fingers together and looked at David with piercing dark eyes.

"Did Puddy . . ?"

"She told me nothing, really. Said she'd leave that to you. But that I'd be interested."

"I, um, don't know how to begin," said David, hesitating.

"When in doubt, it's usually best to do as Lewis Carroll suggested in Alice in Wonderland," the professor said dryly. "Begin at the beginning. Go on until you come to the end. Then stop. And by the way, don't worry about how long it takes. Retired professors aren't very busy people."

"Yes. Well . . ." So David told it again. First, how he and his father had come to be in Wales. The way things were between them. The quarrel. Taking Hywel's motorcycle. Then the accident, and then . . .

The spring evening drew in as he talked. Darkness pooled in the corners of the room, then crept around the two of them, until only the fading glow of the fire lit their faces. Geraint Davies neither moved nor spoke, but sat as he had at the beginning, his eyes fixed on David.

On and on David went, until the story was all told, and his words fell away into silence.

"Fascinating," said the professor, after a few

moments. He added a small piece of coal to the embers in the grate. Then he stood looking out the window for a minute before pulling the curtain across and turning on a lamp. Its glow lit his face strangely from below.

"Your story is a variation I've never heard before," he said, looking across at David. "And I thought I knew them all. You know what I'm talking about, of course?"

"No," said David. "I haven't a clue."

"Ah, yes. You mentioned you didn't care much for school. Didn't ever do much reading, I suppose?"

David shook his head.

"And the names really don't mean anything to you?"

"You mean Meri . . ?" said David, puzzled.

"Not that one. But the others. Bear. Bedwyr. Cai. Even Cabal, the wolf hound."

"Well, I did think Bear was a funny kind of name," said David. "Though it did suit him somehow . . ."

"The word for 'bear' in the ancient Celtic language of Prydein—ancient Britain, to you—is 'artos'," said the professor slowly. "Some people think the name was given to a leader of the British Celts. A very great leader."

He went back to the fireplace and leaned against the mantel, folding his arms across his chest. He fixed his eyes on David. "He's known in literature as King Arthur," he said quietly.

"King Arthur!" David's mouth fell open. "That's . . . that's crazy! Of course I've heard of King Arthur. Knights of the Round Table. All that stuff. But Bear wasn't a king! And Cai and Bedwyr weren't knights! They didn't have shining armour. They didn't even have horses!" He paused a moment, then added, "Well, Lord

Rhodri and his war band did, I guess."

"There's no King Arthur known to history," said the professor. "All that knights of the Round Table—stuff— was invented by poets. But in everything they wrote about Arthur, there is a Sir Bedivere and a Sir Kay. It's as if the poets drew on some old half-forgotten tradition."

"But if there was no king, who was Artos?" asked David.

"He may have been a war leader of the British Celts. Not a king, but someone who led them successfully against the invading Saxons. Someone who won peace for a generation, maybe more. An achievement so great that his name was never quite forgotten. Artos the Bear. He might well have lived in about the period you've described to me. Around 500 A.D."

Bear holding a great sword gleaming red with sunset light.

His own anguished words. *Can't someone stop the dying?*

Bear's eyes widening, his voice saying, *I will.*

And you did. Oh, man, you did it! David thought, with rising excitement. You stopped the killing. And I saw the beginning of it!

Then he remembered the rest of the story, and his elation faded. "He lost though, didn't he, in the end?" he asked.

Professor Davies nodded. "He did. He was betrayed, and the killing times came again. But who knows? Perhaps that space of time he won for peace changed other things. Perhaps the Dark Ages that followed were less dark because of Artos. Perhaps that's why he has never been forgotten."

David let out a long sigh. "But what does it all mean?" he asked, after a moment. "How do I know all these things about . . . Bear. And all the rest?"

"Who can say?" said Professor Davies. "You tell me you've had the dream about the fire for as long as you can remember. That in it you were always looking for something precious that you couldn't find. It's as if your dream were some kind of echo from the past."

"How could it be? Unless—you mean I really lived all that before, but just couldn't remember?"

"Perhaps. There are those who believe such things. Or perhaps that time is still there somewhere, and you went sideways or whatever Emrys said it was. By the way, he's another part of the puzzle. In Welsh he's called Myrddin Emrys. We've always known he was a wise man—a mage and a bard. It's the English who called him Merlin and turned him into a dotty wizard.

"Are you telling me you actually believe me? That you don't think I'm crazy?" David paused, then he blurted out, "You must be crazy too!"

The professor chuckled. Then he shrugged. "I can't accept what you say as historical proof, of course. My training gets in the way. But I'm Welsh, after all. And we're a great people for tales and mysteries. I've spent my life studying the ancient Celts in Wales. And the details you've told me certainly don't sound crazy. In fact they reflect much of what we know."

He thrust his hands deep into the pockets of his old cardigan. "My boy, I'd give ten years of my life to have had an experience like yours. Dream or no. All the things we scholars have wondered about, spun theories about—in some strange way, you've lived it!"

"But I've lost it all, don't you see?" said David bitterly. "I can't get back!"

"Would you go back if you could?" asked Professor Davies.

"I . . ." David hesitated. Would he? Then, "Yes!" he said. "I'd come to care about them all, you see. And there's no-one here I much care about. I don't fit in somehow."

"What makes you so sure?"

"I told you how things were before my dad and I came here. I did a lot of stupid stuff. And when I go home, I'll probably do it again. Or worse."

"Not necessarily. What about your music?"

David looked down at his hands, then he met the professor's eyes. "It's all that holds me together. Always was. But even that's not enough now. Not the way it was before I came here. It . . . it was a shared thing in the. . . dream, you see. It meant something. It wasn't just me sounding off on my own anymore."

"Then why not make your music mean something here? You're a poet, a minstrel. You've just told me so yourself. So why not use what happened to you to make a difference for yourself? And for others."

David was puzzled. "I don't get it."

"You've said that in that other world there was both ugliness and great beauty. There was cruelty, but also loyalty and love. Our world isn't so different. If you were truly a minstrel there, you can be one here."

"You mean . . . use music to say things?"

"Yes! If you want a greener world, why not sing for it? A less violent world? Sing for that, too."

"Oh, sure. A fat lot of difference that would make!" said David.

Professor Davies shook his head impatiently. "A lot, a little, who knows? But music can be a powerful persuader. And if making music is what you're put on Earth to do, then you must do it. You've found out something important about yourself. You can't just turn your back on it!"

Abruptly, he turned and strode out of the room. David wondered if he had offended him somehow, but before he could say anything, the professor returned.

He was carrying a harp, which he set in David's lap.

David's hands trembled as he touched it. It was old and battered-looking. Not nearly as wonderful as Beauty. But a harp. He cradled it on his lap, realizing just how empty his arms had felt these last days.

"It was my wife's. We used to play together before she died," explained the professor, with a nod in the direction of the music stand. "My poor old flute doesn't sound the same without her harp to keep it company." He held out a harp key. "Here," he said. "It needs tuning."

"You want me to play it?" asked David.

"If you dare," replied Professor Davies.

"Dare?"

"You know what it will mean, don't you, if you can play it? Really play it, I mean. Not just start figuring it out."

"That . . . that what happened was real?"

155

"That you can't escape. That you can't go back to your past here any more than to that distant one. That something has changed you, and you have to go forward."

David said nothing. It took him some minutes to tune the harp. Then he settled it against his shoulder and ran his fingers across the strings. His throat suddenly felt dry. He swallowed, then said, simply, "*Culwych and Olwen.*"

He took no time to think but swept into the piece he had played so many times before. He could almost see Lord Rhodri's hall around him. Emrys nodding sternly. Bear and Bedwyr grinning at him. Meri's eyes shining . . .

He finished at last, and came back to himself. He looked across at the professor.

Geraint Davies said quietly, "You can't have learned that here. Not in this century, even. The technique, the style . . . It's amazing! Quite amazing!"

"So now I know."

"Yes. You've been given a great gift, David. The rest is really up to you, isn't it?"

David made to hand over the harp, but the professor shook his head.

"It's yours, if you want it. Oh, you may leave it here for now. You can hardly hump it onto the bus with your crutches and all. But it's yours. Only . . ." He paused, then said wistfully, "Would you come back and play it for me sometimes?"

"I'd like that," said David. "But there's one thing that still bothers me. How can I play rock music on a harp?"

"I've heard it said that love will find a way," said Geraint Davies, smiling.

That night, David lay awake for a long time. If he had to go forward, how should he begin? How could he make his life tight, with no holes for doubt and despair to creep through?

He'd tell his dad he'd stay, of course, even for the extra year his father had planned. How could he leave anyway, still tied to the place by his heartstrings as he was? It wouldn't be easy with his father. But maybe he could make something good come out of it—study music, learn more about the harp.

That was something. But not enough.

He reached over and tugged open the drawer of his bedside table and drew out paper and pencil. He hesitated for a long time. Then, he wrote.

Dear Jamie,

I guess you'll be surprised to hear from me after so long. Maybe you'll tear this letter up. I hope not, though, because I want to say I'm sorry about Jeannie. For what I did. I know just saying that doesn't make it all right. I know it's not that easy. But saying it is where I have to start. I hope someday you'll both be able to forgive me . . .

SEVENTEEN

David returned to school. His father had said he didn't have to. There were only six weeks of term left anyway. But anything was better than sitting alone in their flat. So he went.

It was awkward dragging his way around on crutches. The break had been a bad one, and it would be weeks yet before the cast could come off. But people were kinder than he'd thought they'd be. Someone would hold a door open or offer to carry his books to the next class. Girls he'd found stand-offish now batted their eyelashes and asked him if his leg hurt very much. It was as if stealing something and getting into trouble had made him into some sort of hero. It was kind of embarrassing.

Hwyel, of course, had spread the word about the accident all over the school. Luckily, the bike had not been too badly damaged, and Paul Baird had paid to have it fixed. Hyw boasted that he even got some things fixed that hadn't worked before the accident. David, wincing at the cost, had promised to pay his father back—someday.

"Nicked our Hywel's bike and belted away on up past Abergavenny, I hear," said a boy named Evan Jones, walking beside David as he stumped along on his crutches to their next class.

"Um," said David.

"He did that. Must have been going like a bleeding bat, the coppers said," added another boy. "My da heard it all from one of them and told me. Ran straight into something, you did, though they couldn't figure out what. Lucky to be alive you are, they said."

"Guess I am at that," said David.

"Cor!" said another admiringly. "Didn't think old Hyw's bike had it in it! Bit of a joke that old boneshaker's always been."

David settled into his seat, his leg stuck out at an awkward angle. It was a relief when the teacher arrived.

If I told them I've been running around ancient Britain with King Arthur, they'd say I was nuts, he thought wryly. Even if Professor Davies didn't.

Not much more than a week later, he was standing in the hall half-listening to Evan and the others clowning around. Someone galloped past them down the stairs, heading for the main doors. Out of the corner of his eye, David glimpsed a tall girl disappearing as the doors swung shut. Something about her made his heart leap into his throat.

"Who was that?" he gasped, grabbing Evan by the arm.

Interrupted in the midst of an account of the latest Leeds United-Arsenal match, Evan gaped at him foolishly. "Eh, what?" he asked.

"Someone—a girl—ran down the stairs just then. Did you see who it was?"

Evan shrugged. "Can't say I noticed," he said.

"New girl, that was," said another boy, named Dai. "Transferred in a while back. Right snarky piece, say I. Tried to chat her up, just being friendly and all, and she nearly bit my head off."

"What's her name, though?"

Dai shook his head. "Can't say as I know. She's not in any of our classes. "Anyway, who cares? Keep your distance, that's her motto!"

"Find out, will you?"

"Worth 50p to you, would it be?" asked Dai, grinning.

"Sure, stinker," said David.

"Then I'm your man," said Dai.

As it turned out, David saw her again after school the very next day. Suddenly, she was there ahead of him in the corridor, but before he could struggle through the crowd to her, she had gone out through the front doors.

He dropped his books and swung frantically after her on his crutches. "Meri!" he shouted at the top of his voice. "Meri!"

By the time he came out on the steps, she was halfway across the grounds.

He cupped his hands around his mouth and bellowed, "MERI!" She paused and looked back. Desperately, he waved one arm at her. Then he started hobbling down the stairs. In his haste, he set a crutch wrong, staggered, and almost fell. But he recovered his balance and kept on going.

The girl hesitated, as if she would rather go on. Then she walked back a few steps.

"Meri!" he panted, coming up to her. Then, his heart

sinking, he stopped short and stared. It wasn't Meri. How could he have thought it was? She was tall, like Meri, and broad-shouldered with it. But that was all. Her cropped hair was a coppery red under her peaked cap, and her eyes were hazel-green.

And she was scowling at him. "My name's not Mary. It's Bronwyn Evans. And I don't know you. What d'you mean hallooing after me like that?"

"I'm sorry," said David unsteadily. "For a moment I thought . . . I . . . I . . ." To his horror, he felt his eyes fill with tears.

"Well?" she said. "I haven't time to stand about all day and have you gawp at me, have I? I only stopped because I thought you might fall and hurt yourself. I might have known it was some stupid prank."

"Not a prank," said David unsteadily.

She peered at him. "Here," she said. "You've gone an awful fish-belly colour. You aren't going to faint, are you?"

"It wouldn't be the first time," he managed to say.

She hesitated, then, "You look knackered. Maybe a cup of tea will set you up."

David groaned. These people thought tea cured anything, body or soul!

She ignored his protest. "Just don't think I'm picking you up or anything. It's pure charity. Though you're probably no better than all the other randy lads around here."

She looked down at his leg. "But I guess you can't do too much harm with that whacking great cast on. So come along. There's a place at the corner that'll do."

David nodded, too numb to resist. She turned, and he swung into step alongside her. They crossed the grounds and headed for the corner.

"You must be the twit who stole someone's motorbike and crashed it," she said unsympathetically. "The story's all over the school. What a daft thing to do!"

"It was." David shrugged.

She gave him a sharp sideways glance. "And you've got a funny accent. American, is it?"

"Canadian."

She sniffed, clearly not impressed. "Much of a muchness, I'm sure."

"That's not fair," he shot back. "You Welsh don't much like it when people get you mixed up with the English."

"That's not the same thing," she snapped. "We have our own language and culture and all."

"Ouch!" said David.

A bell tinkled as Bronwyn pushed open the door of the tea shop. "Cream teas for two," she told the waitress, as they settled down at a table. Then, looking David straight in the eye, "I'm starved, happen. But don't worry, I'm paying for my share."

"No, really," he protested. "I'd be glad to pay for us both."

Her full lower lip set stubbornly. "I don't let strange boys treat me to tea, or anything else, thank you very much."

David grinned. He couldn't help it. She was so . . . so . . .

She frowned. "Here, you shouldn't keep staring at me

as if you know me. It's rude. I suppose I look like some girl you know."

He shook his head. "Not really," he said.

"You act daft," she said, with a toss of her head.

"If I told you all about it, you'd know I was daft."

Two furrows of puzzlement appeared between her eyebrows. Then, as the waitress brought their teas, with bowls of clotted cream and jam, and a plate of scones, she shrugged and tucked in.

David ate nothing, but just sat watching her.

"You're not having your tea. Money wasted, that is," said Bronwyn, glancing at him.

You're prickly and impossible, he thought, feeling better than he had for weeks.

"So, go ahead, tell me, then," she demanded, pushing her plate away.

"Tell you what? And you've got jam on your nose."

She dabbed it off with a napkin. "About that girl. What's-her-name."

"Meri. Her name is . . . was . . . Meri. I . . . well, maybe I'd like to tell you about her sometime. But not now. What I want to know is where you come from. I never saw you at school before—I'd remember if I had. And Dai said you were new."

"Is he the one with the fast talk and the busy hands? I sent him off with a flea in his ear, I did," said Bronwyn, a suspicion of a smile lurking at the corner of her mouth.

David laughed. "So he said. But where do you come from?"

"Upriver. Little dot of a place south of Abergavenny."

"Have your people lived there long?"

"Time out of mind, they have," she said. Then added, "Why are you so interested anyway?"

"I . . . I used to have friends up that way," said David. "A long time ago."

She was watching him now, her head cocked on one side and her brows still furrowed. Then she shrugged. "Weird, you are," she said, retrieving her book bag and rootling in it.

David got awkwardly to his feet, fumbling for change for his part of the bill.

The little bell jangled again as they left the shop.

"Well," said David. "See you again, then?"

She tossed her head. "Daresay you will. Seeing that we go to the same school and all."

David swallowed. "I guess what I meant was—would you go out with me again sometime? I'd like to talk to you."

"Well, you'll just have to ask me then, won't you?" she replied. "And we'll see." Her voice was crisp, but the hint of a smile was back at the corner of her mouth.

Just as she was turning away, he noticed what was pinned to the front of her cap. It was a tiny brooch in the shape of an owl. The sparkling stones that were its eyes flashed in the sun. Almost, he thought, as if the owl winked.

And a remembered voice spoke within him. *Fate is a gift, both bright and dark. The wise accept it whole.*

Yes, thought David. Yes, Emrys. You were right after all. Thank you, Lady of Flowers.

He leaned for a moment on his crutches, watching Bronwyn swing away up the street, bag slung over one shoulder, cap set at a jaunty angle. Then he closed his eyes, turning his face up to the May sun. It poured over him like liquid honey. And out of that moment, deep inside him, words and music began to spin themselves into a song.

It wasn't right yet, he told himself. It would take time—maybe a lot.

But then he had that, didn't he?

All the time in the world.

Sharon Stewart was born and raised in British Columbia. She attended Simon Fraser University and did graduate work in London, England and at the University of Toronto. She later taught English for a year in northern China. She now lives in Toronto where she works as a freelance writer, researcher and editor. *The Minstrel Boy* is her first novel for young adults.